The Earl and the Vixen

CHRISTINA DIANE

CHRISTINA
DIANE

The Earl and the Vixen

Unlikely Betrothal Series

Book One

Copyright 2024 by Christina Diane

Edited by Emily Lawrence at Lawrence Editing

Cover Design by Erin at EDH Professionals

eBook ISBN: 978-1-964713-02-1

Paperback ISBN: 978-1-964713-10-6

Contents

Dedicated to all the heartbreak survivors who, for a hot minute, seriously considered burning the world down, but didn't give up on their happily ever after.

Content Warnings

While this particular series isn't heavy on content warnings (but high on spice), I do my best to capture things I think a concerned reader might wish to know. If you ever feel I missed something, please message me on socials or christinadiane@christinadianebooks.com and I will update this list to improve the reading experience for other readers. To prevent spoilers, you can find content warnings for all of my published books here: https://christinadianebooks.com/content-warnings/

Note to Readers

I am so delighted and honored that you have picked up my book! Before you dive in, I would like you to know that I write for the modern reader. My stories are character-driven, fast-paced, and spicy with fun dialogue. While I love the Regency era and exploring the social constructs for the time period, I don't focus on complete historical accuracy. I complete research and attempt to create the setting and behaviors that are close to what you would expect of the era, but sometimes the characters and story have minds of their own. I wouldn't want you to be disappointed if you want a setting, themes, and language that are entirely accurate. If that is really important to you, this book might not be for you. And I understand!

Historical stories are a form of escape and are a fantasy in their own right, and I aim to help bring you to a world that might look and feel very much like the Regency era with diverse, inclusive characters who are fun, sexy, and intriguing as they find their path to love.

If you are excited about hard-headed and swoonworthy gentlemen, spirited and passionate heroines, fun banter, high spice, and guaranteed happily ever afters, set in my interpretation of the Regency era, then I hope you will keep reading and escape into a world of passion, romance, and sharp tongues.

Chapter 1

SURREY, ENGLAND - SPRING 1811

"I love you, Eliza, and I intend to marry you. To hell with our fathers. Please tell me you want to be with me as much as I wish to be with you. In every way."

Elizabeth Nelson, the eldest daughter of the Earl of Nelson, melted into the arms of her sweetheart, Nicholas, who would one day become the Earl of Craven. She had loved him from the first time she'd come across him swimming in the stream that ran between their fathers' estates, almost five years ago.

Although the ownership of that very stream had been a long-disputed issue between their fathers. They each believed that the stream belonged to them and made trouble for each other when either household made use of it for livestock or to provide irrigation to crops. Ultimately, they both ended up using it for their estates anyway, and one would think they could be content with that. But a silly stream had been enough to cause such a rift that the men had sworn to hate each other. The bad blood only became worse between the pair over the years.

When she first saw Nick all those years ago, he hadn't given one whit about her back then. She had been far too young, and he had only been home for the summer from Eton, and by the time fall came again, he was gone. When he returned years later, he came across her reading a novel by the very same stream and finally noticed her, a woman and no longer an annoying young chit. They spent the next few months falling more in love each day and taking a few scandalous swims together at night in the stream in a rebellious slight against their fathers.

There wasn't a doubt in her mind that she wished to marry him, and she wanted nothing more than to give him every part of herself. To truly become his and make him hers. As a young woman of eight-and-ten whom no one spoke of such things to, she knew very little of what that would mean, but she knew she only wished to experience such things with Nick.

He would have offered to marry her already, and they would already be betrothed if they knew for certain how their fathers would react. Given the hatred the men harbored for each other, they feared that Eliza's father wouldn't agree to the union. With her age, they needed his approval to do so properly, or they would have to do something scandalous like elope to Gretna Green.

"I love you, too," she said, burying her face in his neck. "I want very much to be with you, Nick."

He took her mouth with his, kissing her with fervent intensity. When he broke the kiss, he brought her hands to his swollen lips. "Meet me at the hunting cabin tonight, after it is dark. We can be alone there, just the two of us with no one to disturb us."

She looked at their hands, attempting to mask her frown.

"What is it, Eliza? If you have doubts, we can wait," Nick said. He lifted her chin to meet his mesmerizing green eyes. His chestnut hair was just a bit longer than was fashionable, and it made him all the more roguish and handsome. "Look at me. I mean it, if this isn't something you wish to do—"

"It's not that," she said, cutting him off.

"Then is it something I have done? Did you not enjoy when I touched you…" his voice trailed off as he gestured towards her skirts.

"It is most certainly not that either," she said before swallowing hard. She had quite enjoyed it when he introduced her to the most exquisite pleasure she had ever experienced. "It's just that I know you have experienced these things before, and I haven't a clue what to expect or what to do."

Nick had always been honest with her, and he told her of his time at Cambridge and that there had been women who warmed his bed. He spared her the details, which she appreciated, but she wasn't so secure in herself that it didn't spark a flicker of jealousy, especially when she was about to lay herself bare before him.

She knew that the rules of society were different for men than women, especially since Nick was two-and-twenty and exposed to the things men do while at university, but it didn't mean she had to like it.

He cupped her cheek with his hand. "My love, you will be perfect. All I need is you. The rest we can explore together."

"But you—"

"Nothing that happened before you matters," he said, cutting her off, "and I know it isn't fair for me to say so, but I would be driven mad if I had to imagine even the mere notion of another man touching you. If I could change the past, I promise you, I would. Just know that it is of little import to me. You are my future. My everything."

She pressed onto her toes and kissed him again. "I will meet you tonight. I shall have to wait until after Papa goes to bed if I hope to leave." Her papa would not approve of her sneaking out to meet any man, let alone the son of the Earl of Craven. He might have apoplexy if he knew she intended to give Nick her virtue. Papa tolerated Nick's presence when he came to call only because of the politeness society expected. She was certain Papa would refuse him if it wouldn't upset Eliza. Perhaps when she and Nick married, their fathers might resolve things between them. One could only hope.

He brought her hand to his lips again and kissed her knuckles. "You had better return home before someone comes looking for us," he said. "I will see you tonight, my love."

She took his lips again for a few quick pecks and peeked around the corner from the back of her family's stables, ensuring no one could see her as she hurried back towards the house. Her father might tolerate Nick visiting for tea, but if he caught her with him unchaperoned, she wasn't certain she'd see the light of day again. They had to get creative to find ways to sneak off without her maid in tow.

Eliza made it back to the terrace of her grand country home without anyone taking notice. As soon as she entered, she almost walked straight into her father.

"Where have you been, daughter?" he asked.

"I was just taking in the air in the garden, Papa," she lied. She didn't enjoy lying to her father, but she couldn't have him locking her away in her room. Surely love was a reason to justify the minor sin.

His brow furrowed, assessing her. "Where is your maid? You shouldn't be roaming the grounds alone."

"You are quite right, Papa. I just stepped out for a few moments after I was tired of reading. I will make sure Dot goes with me next time," she said, hoping her father wouldn't press her any further.

"Very well. See that you do. Did that boy call here today?"

"Nick?" she asked.

Her father nodded. "And shouldn't you refer to him as Lord Craven?" Hate spewed when her father spoke the title. "You aren't on familiar terms."

Eliza opted not to point out that her father should also refer to Nick by his title and not "that boy," but she opted to leave that unsaid. "Papa, he isn't his father and has done nothing to you. And no, he didn't," she replied. It wasn't exactly a lie since he didn't come calling to their door. "Perhaps he will come for tea tomorrow."

"You are to depart for town with your mama in a few weeks for the season. You are certain to marry before the season ends, so there isn't much point in the boy calling here, I should think," he said, his lips curled into a smirk.

"Perhaps he will offer for me and save you the expense of a season, Papa," she said, testing the waters for her father's reaction.

If she hoped to find a hint of his thoughts on her statement, she would be disappointed. His expression remained unchanged, other than a slight squint of his eyes.

"Perhaps," he said, "but you would have many acceptable options if you had a season."

She patted her father's arm. "The most important thing is that I marry someone who loves me, right, Papa?"

"And someone who is respectable and comes from an excellent family. Someone who would ensure you are provided for," her father said, his cool expression still unchanged.

"Of course, Papa," she replied. "I should like to return to the new book I just purchased with my pin money. May I be excused?" She wasn't ready to tell her father she had already made her choice and would marry Nick. Even if she had to run away with him to Gretna, he was the man she would marry, and there wasn't a thing her father could do about it.

"See you at dinner," her father said before departing towards his study.

Eliza continued to her room, unable to concentrate on reading as her heart wouldn't stop racing. She couldn't wait for her rendezvous with Nick later that evening, where she would learn what it meant to couple with the man she loved.

Around eleven o'clock, Eliza poked her head out of her room to see if anyone was lurking in the hallway. Dot had dressed her for bed a couple hours ago and set her hair into a long plait held in place with a ribbon before she sent the maid away for the evening. Eliza slipped on a serviceable day dress over her night rail and then covered herself with a pelisse to help keep from catching a chill in the cool night air.

Once she was certain there was no one moving about the house, she slipped out of her room and closed the door behind her. She made her way downstairs and snuck out via the door the servants used to access the kitchen garden.

The hunting cabin was only a ten-minute swift ride away, and she knew the route well. With a confident smile, she set off on the journey, assured of her safety under the luminous full moon. She crept to the mews, and a groom greeted her.

"Please saddle up my horse and tell no one that you saw me," she said, handing him a couple of coins.

He pocketed the coins and set off to do as she asked. Jimmy had done so for her a few times before, when she would sneak out to see Nick. The last time they snuck to the hunting cabin, she learnt what an orgasm was. Who knew that a man's hands could give such pleasure? She clenched her thighs together, already thinking about what delights he would introduce her to that evening.

A few moments later, Jimmy handed her the reins, positioning the horse by the mounting block. She thanked him and climbed into the saddle before flicking the reins and racing off into the night.

When she reached the cabin, Nick's horse was already tied up outside. He waited on the porch for her and came right beside her horse and lifted her down. "I'm so very glad you made it, my love. I would have preferred to escort you," Nick said, pulling her into an embrace for a quick kiss. "Let's get you inside. I already started a fire for us."

She grabbed his hand, and he led her inside. The warmth from the fire kissed her skin right away. She removed her pelisse and laid it across the back of the settee. She turned to face him, and in a single fluid movement, he swept her into his arms. Nick pressed his lips to hers, running his tongue along her bottom lip before her lips parted and he massaged her tongue with his. She returned his kiss, sucking his tongue into her mouth until he groaned.

He ambled her backward towards the bedchamber, not breaking their kiss, which grew wilder by the moment. Once inside the room, he kissed her jaw and neck, nibbling at her and then soothing the nips with his tongue.

Eliza sighed, loving the man before her more than she could have thought possible. She glanced around the room and noted he had started a fire in the bedchamber as well, and there were a few candles lit on the mantle above the fireplace.

Nick took her hands in his and leaned back to look at her. His expression was an intoxicating mixture of need and love, and with the light from fire casting shadows on his handsome face, it was an image depicted right out of one of her romance novels. His chestnut hair was almost black in the low lighting and the candlelight hit his green eyes just perfectly so that they shone like a precious gem. She lost her heart to him all over again.

"Are you certain you wish to do this?" he asked, placing a soft kiss on her jaw.

"More than anything," she replied. They had talked about waiting until they were married, but the desire to be with him had consumed her. She couldn't wait for her father to approve her choice. She needed to be with him in every way, and then they would fight for their future together.

A low growl escaped his lips, and he began working the buttons of her dress, unfastening enough that he could lift it over her head and then tossed it on the chair beside the bed.

Curious about what Nick would look like without his clothing, she unbuttoned the coat he wore and pushed it off his shoulders until it fell to the floor. She worked the buttons of his white shirt next. He remained still and allowed her to do as she wished, staring into her eyes as she undid each button and freed him from his shirt.

Her breath caught when she saw his muscular chest with a light smattering of dark hair. When she ran her hands across chiseled muscles and over his shoulders, he sucked in a breath, and the nerves she had about coupling with him evaporated, leaving only raw desire. She kissed his chest, becoming wanton and bold with each press of her lips to his skin. She used her tongue in the same way he did against her neck, and his muscles flexed beneath her touch.

"Eliza, that feels so good."

She licked and kissed his collarbone and up his neck, finding the lobe of his ear. She sucked it into her mouth.

He grabbed her head and kissed her lips again. After a few moments of exploration with their tongues, he broke the kiss and pulled her night rail over her head, leaving her naked before him.

She watched his response to her, and the hunger in his eyes only emboldened her further.

"You are so beautiful," he said, looking from her breasts and down her body. "I must taste you."

She wasn't sure what he meant, but he clasped her bottom and lifted her onto the bed. He tenderly laid her down across the massive bed and positioned himself on his knees between her legs.

He kissed her lips, then kissed his way to her breasts. Her entire body shivered from the sensation of his powerful form hovering over her and the anticipation of what he would do. She gasped when he took one of her nipples into his mouth and began suckling her. "Nick," she cried out.

"Do you like this?" he asked, stopping what he was doing.

"Oh, yes," she replied.

He dipped his head to continue, smiling against her breast every time she moaned or sucked in a breath. When he used his hand to find her nub in the nest of curls between her legs, she moaned again.

He released her nipple and kissed his way down her stomach. He kissed lower and lower, shifting himself further down on the bed until his head was between her legs.

"What are you—" She cried out when his tongue flicked her pearl. "God, yes," she moaned.

He stopped and glanced up at her, a smirk playing on his lips. "Does that mean you wish for me to continue?"

"I may never wish for you to stop."

He gave a smug laugh and flicked her pearl again before circling it with his tongue. He inserted a finger into her core and moved it in and out. Her hands flew to his head, and she undulated against his mouth and hand.

She approached a release similar to the one he gave her a couple of nights ago with his hand, but this was different. Far more intense and wicked. When she tipped over the edge of her climax, she rocked and moaned, calling out his name.

He shifted himself on top of her and kissed her lips. She tasted herself on his tongue and licked the wetness off his lips. It was erotic and exhilarating, and she knew that once would never be enough.

"I could drink from you all day," he said.

"I may wish for you to do just that." She giggled when he laughed at her declaration. "I didn't know such a thing was possible," she said.

He kissed her again. "Would you like to stop now, or would you like for me to show you more?"

"I want more," she replied, the need evident in her tone. "Please, Nick."

Nick climbed off the bed and stood beside it, looking at her.

"Where are you going?" she asked, curving her lips in a playful pout.

"I must remove these now," he replied, working the buttons of his falls, his eyes not leaving hers. He pushed his breeches down to the floor and his member sprang to life, protruding from a nest of dark curls. Her gaze fixed on it, curious about what it might feel like in her hand.

He climbed back onto the bed and hovered over her, placing another sweet kiss on her lips.

"I want to touch you," she said, reaching between them to grasp the rod that stood erect between them.

He sucked in a large breath and closed his eyes when her hand closed around it. Balancing himself with one hand and his knees, he reached his free hand between them and wrapped it around hers. His cock was smooth to the touch but hard as steel.

"You can stroke me like this." He moved her hand with his, and she loved the power she felt from giving him pleasure the way he did for her.

She continued to stroke him for a few moments before he pulled her hand away. "I will spend if you should continue, and I would much rather do so after I make you come on my cock."

She bit her lip, enjoying his wicked words. "Tell me what you are going to do and don't be polite about it."

He slipped his hand between them and slid two fingers inside of her. "I'm going to replace my fingers with the head of my aching shaft, and then I'm going to move like this"—he slid his fingers in and out—"until you shatter and moan in my arms."

She released a sound that was a mixture of a sign and a moan. He pressed his lips to her ear. "Do you want me inside you now?" he whispered.

She nodded.

"Tell me you want me to make love to you with my needy cock," he said, kissing along her jaw.

"I want your cock, Nick," she whispered. "Make love to me. Now."

He withdrew his fingers and positioned himself at her opening. "This may hurt but not for long, and it shouldn't do so ever again."

He pushed himself into her with care, inch by inch. She gasped from the slight twinge of pain when he had his entire length inside of her.

"Are you all right?" he asked.

"Yes," she whispered, the pain subsiding, and she had the urge to move against him. "It doesn't hurt any longer."

He withdrew and then thrust back inside of her, causing her to see stars. She had never imagined such a pleasure and reveled in the intimacy from the man she loved most in the world filling her, the two of them joining as one. Nothing and no one else mattered but the two of them. He did it again, and she cried out.

"That's it, my love. Moan as loud as you wish. It drives me wild to hear you do so."

With every moan, he thrust deeper and harder inside of her. She wrapped her legs around him, and it became even more intense when he entered her as far as he could. He panted and groaned, and she pushed herself against him to meet his thrusts.

"You are mine," he said, thrusting hard and deep.

She responded with a loud moan and dug her fingers into his back.

"Say it," he whispered against her lips.

Eliza kissed him and broke the kiss to speak. "I am yours," she said. "I shall always be yours."

He thrust into her harder and faster.

"Oh, yes," she cried out. "Just like that. Don't stop." With each movement, she neared ever closer to madness and ecstasy. "Nick," she moaned.

He didn't relent and made good on his promise to make her shatter. When she did, she cried out his name again and bucked beneath him, arching her back. Once she rode every wave of the intense pleasure from her climax, he withdrew, his breath ragged. "God, Eliza," he groaned before warm liquid pooled on her stomach.

After a few moments, Nick climbed from the bed and removed a handkerchief from his pocket. He wiped between her legs, then her stomach, and set the handkerchief on the table beside the bed.

"I wiped away the blood, but you may be sore tomorrow. A warm bath should help," he said, settling in next to her and pulling her into his arms.

"That was more wonderful than I imagined," she said, brushing his hair away from his face. "I hope it was the same for you."

He pulled her tighter against him. "My love, I have never experienced anything as intense as being with you. I fear I am addicted to you and shall never get enough."

She giggled beside him. "Is that so?"

"It's perfect since you are mine," he said, kissing her forehead.

"Does that mean you shall meet me here tomorrow night and show me more?" she asked, placing a quick kiss on his chest.

"Nothing on this earth could keep me away."

Chapter 2

S everal nights later, Eliza waited at the hunting cabin for Nick. She did her best to start a fire in the main room of the cabin, but it would need tending once he arrived. Her entire body hummed with need. She recalled the previous evening, when she rode Nick on the very settee where she sat waiting for him. The memory was enough to leave her skin heated and flushed, and her aching for his touch.

She had met Nick at the hunting cabin every night for that entire week. She lost count of how many times he'd brought her over the edge to ecstasy. How many times they had done so for each other. He showed her many delicious and wicked positions for their coupling, and she found she enjoyed licking and sucking his cock almost as much as she enjoyed when he licked and tasted her. She didn't shy away from telling him so, unafraid to voice what she wanted. Besides, he liked when she used words that would be improper to speak to anyone else. Improper to speak at all, as a matter of fact.

In a matter of days, she had become foul-mouthed and wanton, counting the minutes until she would return to the cabin and spend hours in rapture with the man she loved. They were frantic and ravenous, hungry for each other with an intensity that couldn't be tamed. Then afterwards he'd hold her close, and she knew she had found her home in his arms. It was intoxicating and all-consuming, and her desire for him would never be sated.

Last night, they agreed it was time to finally broach the subject of marriage with their fathers. That night, they would discuss when Nick would ask for her father's permission. After he had bent her over the table in the cabin, teasing, tasting, and fucking all of her favorite places first. She licked her lips, and her thighs were already damp from imagining the scene when he arrived.

Eliza only hoped her father would allow her to marry Nick. As a woman of eight-and-ten, she hadn't reached her age of majority and would require her father's legal approval. But if not, they agreed they would run away to

Scotland. She would be Nick's wife soon, with or without her father's permission.

She tapped her fingers on the armrest. Where was he? He was going to pay with his tongue for leaving her waiting. She laughed at the thought, knowing he would be more than happy to oblige her command. The wetness between her legs only intensified with each passing moment, thinking of more and more ways she longed to fuck and make love to him.

Eliza grew more impatient after another hour of waiting. She took to pacing the room if only to keep herself from staring out the window to watch for him.

Another hour passed. Her need had evaporated and she grew worried. Had something happened to him? Panic seized her heart. Hoping he was all right, she stepped out onto the porch of the cabin and listened, in search of any indication that he was on his way to her.

"Where are you, Nick?" she asked to the night sky.

She paced every square inch of the hunting cabin over the course of the next couple of hours until she knew she must return if she didn't wish for anyone to know she hadn't been in her chamber that evening.

Blowing out all the candles before she left, she then mounted her horse and raced back to the mews to toss the reins to the groom and hurry back inside.

When she sank into her bed, she buried her face in her pillow, allowing it to muffle her sobs. What if something happened to him? What if he decided he no longer wished to marry her? No, he loved her. There wasn't a doubt in her mind that he loved her. There had to be some reason he hadn't come to her. He would call on her and explain everything. She was certain of it.

Eliza tossed and turned until the sky began to brighten. She finally passed out from exhaustion, and by the time she opened her eyes again, she hadn't the faintest idea what time it was. The events of the previous evening came flooding back and her heart weighed heavily, worrying about Nick.

Dot knocked and entered her chamber, then set a tray on the table in her chamber. "My lady, you're awake. I tried to wake you earlier, but you seemed to need your rest."

Eliza nodded, massaging her temples from where her head had a dull ache from all the crying she had done and furrowing her worried brow. "I'd like to dress now, Dot."

"Of course, my lady," Dot said. "I have a morning dress pressed and ready for you."

Dot helped her to dress and styled her hair into a simple chignon. Eliza didn't have the energy to carry on conversation, and she wasn't certain if Dot attempted to speak to her. She could only think of Nick. Dot encouraged her to eat a few bites of the food from the tray, but Eliza's stomach was in knots, and she couldn't think of food when something may have happened to Nick.

She departed her chamber, attempting to form a plan to go to his father's home to see about his welfare. She would have no choice but to seek assistance from her father. Perhaps it was time she told her father of her intention to marry Nick and he just might understand and aid her. She set off towards his study, hoping she might find him there.

The door was open, and when she peeked her head in, she found him sitting at his desk.

"Papa?" she called out to get his attention, crossing the threshold to enter the room.

"Eliza, there you are," he said, rising from his seat. "This came for you."

She eyed the missive in her father's hand and released a long breath. A bit of relief washed over her. It must be from Nick. He wrote to explain what had occurred and all would be well. She took the letter from her father and inspected the writing on the outside. Her name was written in a neat but masculine hand.

She broke the seal and began reading the words to herself.

Lady Elizabeth,

I know you harbored hope that we would marry, but I must inform you that this notion shall never come to pass.

There is too much bad blood between our families to make a marriage between us work. Surely you are already aware of this.

Perhaps if I truly loved you, it would be enough. But alas, that was never the case. Although, it was fun making you believe so. I could never love the daughter of my father's sworn enemy.

Lord Nicholas Craven

Tears streamed down her cheeks, and she fought to keep from casting up her accounts. She gripped the edge of her father's desk to steady herself and keep from sinking to the floor.

"What is it, Eliza?" her father asked.

She shook her head, unwilling to look at her father.

"Give that to me now," he commanded. He held his hand out, waiting for her to comply.

With no choice, she handed the missive to her father, hanging her head in shame.

Her father shook his head and crumpled the parchment before letting it drop to the ground.

"I knew that boy would be trouble," he spat. "His father must have put him up to toy with you. Be glad you are rid of him."

Her chest heaved as she tried to catch her breath, and her knuckles were white from how hard she continued to grip the side of the oak desk. "He wouldn't, Papa. He does love me. Something must be wrong."

"How much more proof do you need?" her father challenged, waving his hand towards the parchment on the floor. "I told you he was no good and that his presence would only cause you harm. He is as entitled and useless as his father. Better that you learnt the truth now."

Eliza's thoughts muddled and she struggled to accept what was right in front of her face. She could hardly see from how hard she sobbed.

She wiped her eyes and swallowed hard. "May I be excused, Papa? I wish to return to my chamber."

His expression softened, and he patted her shoulder. "Of course."

When her father returned behind his desk, she quickly grabbed the crumpled parchment from the floor and fled the room. She didn't slow her pace until she was on the other side of her locked chamber door.

She smoothed the parchment and read it over and over, again and again. Eliza didn't want to believe it was true, but how could she not? Nick hadn't shown up at the hunting cabin and hadn't called on her that day. He would have appeared to her if there was a mistake. But the coward couldn't even face her, instead sending a note to break her heart and make her wise to what he was truly about.

How had she been such a fool? She fell for every one of his hollow words, believing that he loved her. She had been nothing but a game to him. A way to lash out at her family because of the bad blood between their fathers. A way to use her body to sate his own needs until he had tired of doing so. He'd tell everyone how he bedded her, fucking her in every way imaginable, and she'd be ruined.

One thing was certain: she wasn't stepping foot in London for the season. Why bother? If all that had transpired had taught her anything, it was that she would be better off without a husband. Although, if she were honest with herself, she wished to avoid encountering Nick. If she had to be in his presence again, there was no telling what she might do to him. Part of her longed to rip him to shreds.

The other part of her, however, longed for understanding. Longed to believe there was a part of him that loved her. It couldn't have all been an act, could it? He may not love her, but even her pride couldn't get her to pretend she didn't love him. And as long as she still harbored any love for him, she couldn't face him. She couldn't be trusted to think with sense and for every fiber of her being not to want him. It was clear she would need more time than she cared to admit to stop loving that vile, wretched bastard.

Chapter 3

NORFOLK, ENGLAND - SEPTEMBER 1814

Eliza allowed the footman to hand her down from her father's carriage, with her maid, Dot, following behind her. She glanced up at the opulent country home of Viscount and Viscountess Ockham. The house would be her home for the coming fortnight, along with around thirty other guests. Her hosts decided to hold a big house party since they weren't in town for the season due to the birth of their child. It would appear that they had decided to go all out and make it a large event. And knowing her hostess, the party wouldn't be dull.

Moments after her feet hit the ground, the fiery viscountess greeted her. "I am so glad you could join our house party, Lady Eliza. I do hope you enjoy the entertainment I have planned," the lady said.

"Thank you for the invitation, my lady," she returned. "I have been looking forward to it."

Lord Ockham reached his wife's side and wrapped his arm around her waist. Eliza formed a tight smile, fighting not to roll her eyes. The couple was notoriously a love match, and their outward display of affection was enough to make her gag. They were a striking couple as well, both with dark hair and piercing eyes, which only made their perfect love all the more irritating, even if she did like them both very much.

Even though she enjoyed the couple, she had long given up on the belief that love was real. Three years of living in the torture and pain left in the wake of Nick's cruel treatment of her was a constant ongoing reminder that would dissuade her of any notion that she might give what little was left of her heart to another man. She tried that once, giving everything she had, including her virtue, to Nick before he crushed her heart into tiny pieces and threw them back in her face.

"Good to see you, Lady Eliza," Lord Ockham said, bowing to her.

"Same to you, my lord," she replied. "Your home is lovely."

Lady Ockham motioned to a man who appeared to be their butler. "Baxter," the viscountess said, "please show Lady Eliza to her chamber and coordinate the delivery of her trunks." She shifted her attention back to Eliza. "I put you in the room next to Lady Juliet. She arrived a quarter hour before you. Once you are settled, we will all gather in the salon at six sharp before dinner is served."

"Thank you, my lady," Eliza replied. "I shall see you shortly."

Eliza was relieved that Juliet had already arrived. Lady Juliet Lane, the daughter and only child of the Earl of Avon, had become one of her closest friends when she attended her first season in London. The two of them each had their reasons for shying away from the gentlemen of society. Juliet was the one person she had trusted with her biggest secret, that she had given her maidenhead, among other things, to the most despicable gentleman of society. Although, given that he'd never shown his face at any *ton* events, perhaps he wasn't a member of society after all.

The belief that he was too much of a coward to face her gave her a small sense of satisfaction. She hadn't heard word that he had died, so she hoped he was somewhere, afraid of what she might do to him if she ever saw him again. She heard from her papa that Nick's father had passed over a year ago, not that her father was displeased to hear the news. That meant Nick had become the Earl of Craven and could pick up the battle over the stream, like the bacon-brained dolt he was. The feud over a body of water had been enough to make her collateral damage. That was all her love and virtue had been worth to the man.

As much as she tried to push him from her thoughts, she surmised that he should be out of mourning. The last time she laid eyes upon the blackguard, he spoke of his undying love for her. Granted, he had just come on her tongue mere moments before he said so. The man should have taken to the stage, given the skill he possessed to make one believe he felt things he didn't.

Eliza gritted her teeth, recalling the memory of them lying across the settee together. She forced herself to focus on her surroundings as she made her way up the staircase behind Baxter. She could almost smell the cedar and bergamot scent she would forever associate with him. She thought of him far more frequently than she cared to admit, even all the years later. He had become a sickness she would never recover from, no matter how hard she tried.

"Eliza! You are finally here!" Juliet called to her, standing in the doorway of the room they passed by.

"You will be in this room," Baxter said, motioning to the doorway beyond where Juliet stood.

Eliza thanked him, and he retreated towards the staircase. Juliet approached her and they bussed each other's cheeks. Eliza's friend pulled her into the room where Juliet was staying, and they each took their seats in chairs by the fireplace.

"This is going to be a fun fortnight," Juliet said. "I can't believe both of our mamas let us come without them."

"Well, it may not be the case for you at nine-and-ten, Jules, but I am practically a spinster. Mama had no concerns about sending me on my own," Eliza said.

Juliet swatted her forearm. "Don't say such things. One-and-twenty does not make you a spinster, and you aren't unmarried because you lack options," Juliet reminded her. "You turned down another proposal just last month."

Eliza laughed. "I do not insult myself. I have no intention of marrying. You know that. I am quite content."

"Is that so?" Juliet asked, a knowing arch to her brow.

"I am," Eliza insisted. "I mean, sure, I might like to experience the physical nature of a man's company, but marriage isn't required to do so. Obviously." Eliza's unfortunate encounter with Nick had been proof of that. She would read his letter again later to remind herself of the very thing. She brought it with her everywhere she went when she needed a reminder of how cruel men could be.

31

And as much as she hated to admit it, the desire for the things that she and Nick did together lingered just below the surface, waiting for her to give herself leave to experience them again.

"Yet you haven't done so with anyone else," Juliet said.

It annoyed Eliza to no end when Juliet pointed out that fact. Eliza wasn't certain why she hadn't attempted to take another lover. She contemplated it over the years, but she hadn't been bold enough to be so vulnerable with another man. Nor had she found the opportunity, in truth. Until the house party invitation, she always had her mother with her at all the events she attended. There weren't any other neighbor boys who might sneak over to fuck her and pretend they loved her, like the last one did.

Eliza rapped her fingers on the armrest, a habit her mother would chastise her for. "Perhaps I'll do so while we are here." She wasn't certain she would, but the idea of an orgasm that didn't come from her own hand certainly held appeal.

Juliet smirked. "Well, house parties are perfect for slinking off with a handsome gentleman. I am certain you won't be the only one doing so."

"I heard that Lady Preston shall be in attendance," Eliza said. "She is almost certain to take a lover." The lady had lost her husband around three years ago and had developed a bit of a reputation for avoiding marriage but enjoying bringing men to her bed, among other places. Eliza supposed she couldn't blame the lady.

"Should we take bets on who she shall select?" Juliet asked.

Eliza's jaw dropped. "Jules!" Then a sly expression formed on her face. "Well, perhaps we shall see who pays her attention this evening and make our guesses."

Juliet bit her bottom lip. "This is going to be fun, indeed."

Eliza flashed a wide grin at her friend. Perhaps Juliet was right, and it was time she considered bringing another man to her bed. Marriage and love were out of the question, but she couldn't allow herself to go the rest of her life without experiencing the wicked touch of a man again, could she? She had been naïve and lovesick then, but she had become a mature woman who knew what she wanted. She couldn't give Nick the satisfaction of robbing her of carnal pleasures, especially after he thoroughly exposed her to the existence of such delights.

A smirk played on her lips. Perhaps Lady Preston wouldn't be the only one assessing the men that evening. Surely someone would be in attendance who might intrigue her.

Chapter 4

E arl Nicholas Craven fixated on the fire in the bedchamber that the Ockhams had assigned to him at
their country home. He wasn't certain it had been the
best idea to attend at all, but he couldn't insult his hosts
now that he had arrived. The Viscountess Ockham was
intimidating, even as young as she was. She'd surely see
through any excuse he made to leave.

Nick avoided any event where there might be a chance
of him seeing Eliza again. After what had passed between
them, he had no desire to find himself in her presence
ever again. He avoided the season in London, knowing
that he couldn't avoid her in ballrooms with the entire *ton*
present.

He wasn't aware that she had any association with Lord and Lady Ockham, and it had been years since he had seen his friend Ockham. The two had gotten into a bit of mischief from time to time when they were at Cambridge, and Ockham wished for Nick to attend the gathering to meet his wife. She was a lovely woman, and the pair were an obvious love match.

Nick rolled his eyes. Love. What a farce. If he hadn't seen for himself how enamored Ockham and his wife were with each other, he'd say that love didn't exist at all. It was certainly not in his future. He wasn't certain he even cared to ever take a wife. Why bother saddling himself with a woman when he knew he'd never feel anything for her? What did he care about providing an heir? Surely there was some cousin or distant relative the title could pass to. They would be delighted to elevate themselves in society, and he would never have to suffer the agonizing notion of courtship.

He did that once and didn't care to again. It wasn't like he couldn't have a woman in his bed anytime he wished. As a titled gentleman with ample funds, there wasn't much he couldn't have if he desired it. Other than love. Never that.

The love of his life rejected him and married another man. His father broke the news to him after he spent months pining for her, longing to see her and make her remember that she loved him. Even broken-hearted, he hadn't been able to bring himself to fuck anyone else, which furthered the cruel madness that had become his life. He tried several times, paying for the company of a faceless woman, hoping to cure himself of the hold that the love of his life held on his heart and apparently his body.

It was the same thing every time. He would partake of a few drinks and then when he thought he had worked himself up enough to finally stick his cock in another woman's mouth, cunt, or arse—he told himself he didn't care which—he would back out at the last minute. Retreating to his rooms to fuck his own hand. Thinking about her. It was beyond pathetic, and he'd never live down the shame if anyone knew. He wasn't certain what would cure him, but he longed for the day he would free himself from the torment.

Nick gritted his teeth and found he was beyond ready to find the nearest snifter of brandy.

He glanced at the clock on the mantle and decided he should make his way downstairs. His hostess said six sharp for his presence downstairs and he wouldn't dream of facing her wrath should he arrive late.

Nick departed his chamber and descended the grand staircase until he reached the salon where others were gathering. The sun was setting on the horizon outside the glass doors, which led to a large terrace. There were several guests already mingling, and the low buzz of conversation could be heard as soon as he entered. Immediately spotting his hosts, he crossed the room to greet them.

"I am glad to see you are punctual, my lord," the viscountess said.

Ockham pushed a glass of brandy into his hand, casting him an amused grin.

"Your husband has already informed me I shouldn't cross you, my lady."

She patted his arm. "I know you and my husband have been friends for many years. He speaks fondly of your days at university, and I even heard you spent some time together in Italy."

Nick laughed heartily. "Those were fun times, indeed. Ockham wrote that he took you to see some of the places we visited."

Lady Ockham looped her arms through her husband's and looked up at him with nothing but love, and Nick was thankful she wasn't looking at him to see how he rolled his eyes.

"That he did," she said. "We visited for a year after we married, then returned home so we could have our son back here at home."

"Congratulations to you both. I hope to meet him while I am here," Nick said, taking a large swig of his drink.

"What about you, old man?" Ockham asked, slapping Nick on the back. "Surely you are thinking about leg shackling yourself in the near future?"

Nick choked on the second swig of brandy he took and patted his chest with his fist.

"I'm not so sure about that, old friend," Nick said.

Lady Ockham clasped her hands together. "Oh, I'd be happy to give my opinions on the young ladies present at the party. Perhaps you shall meet someone while you are here."

The woman was far too excited by the notion of matchmaking, and Nick shook his head in response. "That isn't necessary. I have much to do with my estates, and a wife would just get in the way."

Ockham audibly sucked in a large breath of air, and his wife cast her husband an annoyed sideways glance before refocusing her attention on him.

"That is the most bacon-brained thing I have ever heard," she said before glancing at her husband again, "and I have heard some bacon-brained things."

Based on the hard expression on her face, Nick wouldn't dare to ask but chuckled to himself imagining what might have earned his friend such ire.

"Now, now, my love," Ockham said, kissing his wife's temple, "I'm sure what Craven means to say is just that he isn't ready to take a wife yet. Give him just a bit of slack, my love, the man had his heart broken."

"Ockham," Nick ground out. "Don't." The last thing he wished to do was discuss the greatest heartbreak of his life in the middle of a country house party. Or ever.

The viscountess patted his arm, and pity washed over her expression. "I'm so sorry, my lord. I didn't know. What happened?"

"She married someone else," Nick said, downing the rest of his brandy. Ockham reached for the decanter and refilled Nick's glass with a healthy pour, and he immediately downed that, too.

"Who is she?" Lady Ockham asked. "I shouldn't like to associate with someone who would hurt my husband's dear friend in such a way. You will find that we are quite loyal to our friends."

"My love," Ockham replied, saving Nick from having to answer. "He will never tell you. I tried to get it out of him over many drinks, and he won't budge."

Nick exhaled hard. "He's right, my lady. I adore you already, but that pain is mine to carry, and that's that."

The viscountess huffed but didn't press further. Although he wasn't certain he'd be so fortunate for the entire fortnight.

"Very well," she said. "I'm still going to think about which ladies might make a good match for you in case you change your mind."

Ockham laughed. "My wife is nothing short of relentless."

"I see that," Nick deadpanned. He could only hope she'd get distracted with marrying off more willing guests and leave him be.

"My love," she said, "we should greet some of our other guests."

"Of course. Craven, you should mingle with the others, too. You haven't been seen in society in a couple of years. It would do you some good."

Nick nodded and watched his hosts move to another group of guests.

He reached for the decanter on the sideboard next to where he stood and refilled his glass. He turned around to see if he recognized any of the other guests in attendance so he might do as Ockham suggested and re-acquaint himself.

A pair of ladies entered the room, and he glanced at them from the side of his eye and then did a double take. His throat went dry, and his heart was in his throat.

If lightning had struck him where he stood, he would have been less jarred than by the woman he had fixed his gaze upon. No, surely it couldn't be that the one person he never wished to encounter again had just entered the salon, where he would be unable to go unnoticed by her.

His entire body tensed and his hands formed tight fists. He groaned to himself, and his jaw clenched so hard that it hurt. His cock twitched as well, but he refused to give that even the faintest bit of attention. Eliza.

After the way things ended between them, fate must be playing a cruel joke or some kind of retribution for trapping him for an entire fortnight with her. Hadn't he already suffered enough? He was a step away from being a monk, and there she was tempting and teasing him, reminding him of what he lost. What she stole from them both.

He found himself unable to look away from her, and he hated himself for it. She was even more beautiful than the last time he'd seen her, with a few loose curls of her caramel-colored hair framing her heart-shaped face. Her body appeared even more womanly, and it did nothing to ease the strain in his breeches, as well as the anger boiling beneath the surface.

Before he could force himself to look away, her eyes met his. She attempted to school her features, but her crystal blue eyes failed her. If the ire in her expression was any indication, the lady was just as unhappy to see him as he was to see her, which wasn't at all surprising.

After what had occurred between them, he was certain she didn't wish to be in his presence. The feeling was entirely mutual, but it would appear they were stuck. They would be forced together for an entire fortnight, required to put on airs and polite niceties for the benefit of the other guests.

Although he supposed it shouldn't be difficult for her given her ability to trick and mislead others. Perhaps he might finally force her to explain herself. At least if he could leave the house party with matters resolved and the ability to fuck again, that would be a start. He'd certainly never love again.

He raised his glass to her with a tight smile, as if he toasted the wordless pact he'd made to move on from her, then took a healthy gulp.

She whispered something to the lady beside her and then started right for him. *Hell and damnation.* Nick wasn't ready, as he hadn't prepared for that moment. What would he even say to her? He hadn't even imagined the situation because he never intended to subject himself to it. Part of him wanted an explanation in the hope of releasing himself from her hold, but the other part of him worried he might lose the other half of his soul hearing the words aloud. Suspecting she never loved him and hearing her say it were two different things entirely.

She held her chin high and didn't take her eyes off his as she approached.

"Lord Craven," she said, the disdain evident in her tone. "I didn't expect to see you here."

He drained the remaining contents of his glass. It hardly seemed necessary for her to state the obvious.

"I'm sure you are just as delighted as I am about this revelation," he said, matching her tone.

"Quite," she spat. "I should have known that I couldn't avoid your unwelcome presence forever."

At least she kept her voice low, so perhaps they wouldn't have their row where the entire room could bear witness. It was bad enough to live the shame, but he certainly didn't wish the rest of society to know how lost he had been to the woman in front of him.

"The feeling is indeed mutual," he returned, flashing her a tight, fake smile. He pretended to look around the room. "Where is your husband? Certainly he should keep an eye on you."

She scoffed. "That's low. Even for the likes of you and the very low standard one might hold you to. And not that it is any of your business, but I am here alone."

"Oh, hoping to partake of a willing gentleman," he said, waving his hand towards the other guests. "I'm sure there will be many options at a country house party for a light skirt such as yourself. Please don't let me keep you." He didn't mean that in the slightest. The same as he couldn't allow another woman in his bed, the idea of her fucking another man was far too much for him to handle. Knowing she had married and another man climbed on top of her made his skin crawl and was the source of his nightmares.

She stepped closer to him and lowered her voice even further, speaking through her teeth. "You are a cruel bastard. Stay away from me." She turned on her heel and crossed the room to rejoin her friend.

How dare she treat him like he was the cruel one after what she had done? How she ran off and married someone else without a glance back or even a conversation with him? Nick had loved her more than he had ever believed possible. He would have destroyed the entire world and watched it burn if that would have been what was required to have her. He would have laid down his life for hers if the need had presented itself. And she went and married someone else. Then there she was, flaunting herself around at house parties without her husband, whomever the poor cuckold was, in tow.

"Nick, good to see you," a familiar voice said, pulling him from his disdain for the frigid woman of his past.

"Onslow," Nick said, "it's been a long time." Hudson Brooks, the Earl of Onslow, was another friend from his days at Cambridge.

"I heard you lost your father a while back," Onslow said. "Please accept my condolences."

"Same to you. I heard about your parents. I can't imagine losing both at once," Nick replied.

The man frowned. "Indeed. It's been a few years now, but I have learnt to adjust."

"I guess we have no other choice. It is what is expected, I suppose," Nick said.

Eliza's laugh caught his attention. It was like the tinkling of bells, and he pushed away a memory of her giggling in his arms after one of the many times they had made love. Well, at least for him it had been love. She seemed to be incapable of the emotion. He tamped down his rage that she was speaking with a gentleman who glanced at her chest when the man believed Eliza wouldn't notice. Worse, why did he even care? She probably welcomed the attention.

"Do you fancy Lady Eliza?" Onslow asked, a knowing smirk playing on his lips.

"What? No," Nick replied. "And shouldn't you refer to her by her married name?"

Confusion marred the man's expression. "What are you talking about?"

"Wasn't she married a few years ago? Or is she a widow now?" Nick asked. That would explain why she had attended the house party on her own if she were, in fact, a widow. And why she would consider throwing herself at the likes of Lord Irvine.

"I think you are confused from your time away from society, Nick," Onslow said. "Lady Eliza has never married. She has turned down countless proposals. Her name is on the betting books at White's, with many hoping to win her hand."

The color drained from Nick's face. She hadn't married. How could that be? His father very clearly told him she had married. There was no mistaking that. He never cared to ask who she had wed and had no reason to believe his father would lie to him. He left for Italy the next day to join Ockham on his tour. Why would his father lie?

"Are you all right, Nick?" Onslow asked.

He shook off his thoughts. "Of course," Nick replied, almost certain his tone wasn't enough to convince his friend. "Are you one of the men hoping to win her hand?"

"Afraid not. I'm not ready for the leg shackle, but good luck to you if you intend to enter the melee. From the number of rejections she's meted out, you're going to need it," Onslow said, laughing heartily before taking another large swig of his drink, then continued. "She could be a character in one of those Stormy Wells plays the *ton* can't seem to get enough of."

"Stormy Wells?" Nick asked. What was the man talking about?

Hudson laughed. "You really should visit Town more often, Craven. I don't fancy the balls, but exhibits at the museum and a trip to the theater are a nice break from solitary country living."

"I'll give it some thought," Nick replied, not fully listening to the man.

Eliza laughed again, and the gentleman she spoke to leaned far closer to her than he should have. The intense urge he had to pummel the man wasn't lost on Nick. If the man laid a single finger on her, he just might do so. He would get to the bottom of why his father lied to him about Eliza. He reminded himself that regardless, she still pushed him away. She abandoned him and refused to see him. And for some unknown reason, she appeared to hate him as much as he had hated her for doing so, which was laughable.

Chapter 5

Eliza closed and locked her door, securing herself inside her chamber, finally free from Nick's presence. She couldn't help but glance at him throughout dinner, and every time she did, he stared back at her. His presence drove her to distraction. Heat pooled between her thighs, and the dampness from her wet core caused her to shift in her chair throughout dinner.

She flirted with Viscount Irvine, who had been seated next to her during the meal. He was a notorious rake, but at least if she selected him to release the building tension with a bit of physical attention, he wouldn't try to convince her to marry him. She had to be careful who she selected for such an endeavor because if the gentleman wished to wed her badly enough, all he would have to do was threaten her reputation.

Digging through her trunk, she found Nick's letter. She read it to herself and then read it again for good measure. She needed to remind herself why they would never be, and it was all his fault. He threw her away, lying and tricking her.

There was a soft knock at the door, and Eliza's breath caught. She tucked the letter back into her trunk, too embarrassed to let anyone know that she carried it with her. That she still needed to read it, and often.

"My lady," Dot said, from the other side of the door. "Shall I help you ready yourself for bed?"

She unlocked the door and allowed Dot to enter. Once Eliza was out of her gown and dressed in her night rail, Dot brushed and plaited her hair.

As soon as Dot took her leave for the evening, Eliza locked the door again. She wasn't sure if she thought she was locking others out or attempting to lock herself in.

Nick was even more handsome, which she wouldn't have thought possible. His skin was slightly more tan than she remembered and his shoulders were broader. She wondered if his muscles were still just as taut beneath his coats. They certainly appeared as if they had grown larger. She hated that she'd noticed and even more so that her notice brought her wanton needs even closer to the surface.

She climbed into the bed and stared at the top of the canopy that covered the large four-poster. She closed her eyes and his naked chest flooded her thoughts again. Forgetting about the letter and the reminder of his cruelty, the throbbing between her legs became almost unbearable. She imagined him licking his full lips before he positioned himself to kneel between her legs.

Grasping the side of her night rail, she pulled it up so that her wet heat was exposed to the cool air of the room. Eliza ran her hands down her body until she reached the places where she imagined his tongue might explore. She used her fingers and imagined Nick's tongue circling and flicking her pearl where she touched herself. She increased her pace and used her other hand to slip two fingers inside of herself, fantasizing that the fingers were Nick's.

As she came closer to her release, she bit her bottom lip to keep from crying out and rocked her hips against her hands until she claimed every second of pleasure from her climax. She dropped her hands to her sides and worked to return her breathing to normal.

She had imagined similar scenes many times over the years. She told herself she fantasized about Nick every time because he was the only man she had made love to, fucked, sucked, licked, and everything in between. But the intensity of her orgasm outed her as a liar. None of that could happen again. Nick was cruel and never cared for her. He didn't deserve her thoughts or her desire, even if he wasn't aware that she desired him still. She could only imagine the haughty look he'd give her if he knew she allowed him to fuck her in her fantasies.

Perhaps she should consider a tryst with the handsome Lord Irvine in earnest. She needed her urges to be sated and soon if she had any hope of preventing Nick from consuming her every thought.

"What is this mood of yours?" Juliet asked the next morning, her eyes fixed on Eliza as she moved about her chamber. She attempted to appear as if she were looking for something, when in actuality she hoped to delay being in Nick's presence again.

Eliza huffed. "I'm not in a mood. It is a perfectly delightful day."

Juliet laughed at her, causing Eliza to roll her eyes in annoyance that her friend was far too accurate for her liking, but she didn't wish to explain why sleep didn't come easy for her the previous evening. Or why she would suggest they took trays in her room if she thought her friend would agree to the notion.

"You could just tell me what is troubling you," Juliet pressed.

"I didn't sleep well. It's nothing of import." She glanced over at her friend and saw the look of disbelief spread across her face. "I am just looking for my hair clip, and we can depart." Dot had already tended to Eliza's hair, which she expected Juliet to quickly point out.

To her surprise, and gratitude, Juliet accepted the excuse and didn't press her further. She used the quiet in the room to center her thoughts and prepare herself for seeing Nick again. It was an inconvenience they would both have to accept, and she could only hope it irked him even more than it had her.

Deciding she couldn't prolong the inevitable any longer, she grabbed a hair clip from her vanity and pressed it into her hair.

"Very well. Let's join the others downstairs."

"I will get you to tell me what this is about," Juliet said as they exited Eliza's chamber.

"I told you…"

"And I don't believe you."

Eliza couldn't be all that irritated since her friend was right. She would tell her about Nick later when she was ready to speak of the matter. Juliet would be introduced to him sooner or later, so she couldn't keep her secret for much longer.

They made their way to the breakfast room in silence, their arms looped together. Eliza's heart stopped when she saw Nick sitting with some of the other gentlemen at the table. She glanced away as soon as he noticed her, not in an attempt to play some sort of game of hard-to-get, but to ensure Juliet didn't take notice.

Going straight to the sideboard, they each prepared their breakfast plates. Eliza wasn't all that hungry, but she wouldn't give the liar sitting at the breakfast table the satisfaction of thinking for even a moment that he had affected her to such an extent.

When they had finished making their selections, Eliza nudged Juliet to the other end of the table, taking their seats as far away from Nick as she could get them. Viscount Duncan followed them and took the seat on the other side of Juliet.

The upside to the gentleman joining them was that he spoke to Juliet and kept her friend's attention. Anything to keep Juliet from asking her why she pushed her food around on her plate or why her mood hadn't improved.

"I do hope you won't mind my company, my lady," a man's voice said from her right.

Lord Irvine dropped into the empty seat beside her.

"Not at all, my lord," she returned, shifting her full focus to the broad-shouldered, attractive man. If she were going to consider taking another to her bed, he would certainly be a pleasing option.

"You look lovely this morning if you will allow me to say so," he said, the words rolling off his tongue smoothly.

She fought a smirk, smart enough to know that he was employing his rakish charms on her. Instead, she flashed him a demure grin. "I would hardly turn down a compliment from a handsome gentleman."

He had a cocky air to his response, and she contemplated deflating the man's ego just a bit. But it would suit her if she decided to entertain more physical things with him. The man would at least have enough experience to make it worth her while. Her cheeks reddened at the thought of such wicked things, and she hated how her thoughts flashed back to Nick.

It was a wise choice on her part to ensure they sat on the same side of the table as him, if not she might have looked down the table to catch a glimpse of him. But if she attempted to do so in their current seating arrangement, all she would see would be Juliet and Lord Duncan.

Lord Irvine droned on about some of the latest *on dit* about some of their mutual acquaintances until it was time for all the guests to make their way out to the yard for games. Once they had all assembled, everyone shifted their focus to their hostess.

"I want everyone to pair off in teams for a game of Pall Mall. There will be a prize for the winning team," Lady Ockham explained to everyone who had formed a circle around her in the grass.

Unable to stop herself, Eliza glanced at Nick out of the corner of her eye, half expecting him to be watching her as he had done the previous evening. She fought the twinge of jealousy when she noted he was in conversation with Lady Preston.

She was a beautiful blond widow, and Nick already appeared far too familiar with her. Not that she cared. He was nothing to her, and he could do whatever he wished. It was of no matter to her if he took up with the lady.

In a moment that she refused to admit was jealousy, Eliza noted Lord Irvine standing nearby and caught his attention with a sultry grin.

"Would you do me the honor of partnering with me, my lady?" he asked, stepping closer to her.

She almost laughed out loud at how easy it had been to lure him in.

"I would be delighted, my lord." She grinned up at him through her lashes.

She glanced back at Lord Irvine and caught him staring at her chest. Deciding to toy with his notice, she inhaled slowly, causing her chest to rise. Eliza smiled to herself when he licked his bottom lip. It wouldn't be the least bit difficult to hold the man's attention if she should want it.

Lady Ockham caught everyone's attention again. "Everyone line up here and select your mallet. You will share with your partner, taking turns for each swing. The first team to get their ball through the final wicket shall be the winners."

"Please, select for us, my lady," Lord Irvine said, motioning towards the stand of mallets. There were eight total couples playing, while a group of spectators watched from under the cover of tents.

Eliza noted that Juliet had been paired with Lord Duncan and wondered if her friend might have an interest in the gentleman. Eliza would speak with her about the man later. She didn't care for the way he ogled her friend when she wasn't looking, and she heard many rumors about his gambling debts. He wasn't for her friend if she thought to make a match with him.

Stepping up to the rack, she looked over the mallets and grabbed the red one, right as Lady Preston selected the purple one from beside her.

"I hope you won't mind purple, Nick, but it is my favorite color."

Eliza did her best not to scoff and roll her eyes at the lady, noting that Nick had already given her leave to use his given name. In truth, she took no issue with Lady Preston, normally, but she struggled to tamp down her desire to wipe the smile off the lady's face.

Eliza spun back towards Lord Irvine. "I got us red, my lord. It's such a passionate color, is it not?" she asked, looping her arm in his so he could escort her to the first wicket. Cheesy at best, and she should be embarrassed of herself, but it was all she could come up with, with so much rage coursing through her. She told herself again that it wasn't jealousy, just the residual rage that was well within her right to have after a man used lies and charms to get between your legs.

"I quite agree," he said, leaning down so he spoke close to her ear, heating it with his breath.

Eliza noted that she had no reaction to the man, which irritated her almost as much as being in Nick's presence. Irvine was handsome, to be sure, with his dark chestnut hair and intense eyes almost the same color, but her body felt nothing.

There was no electricity or draw like she had from the moment she saw Nick emerging from the stream that day years ago, water dripping from his taut form. But eventually, she must will her body to move on from the memories.

She shook off her thoughts and glanced back at Nick. That time he met her gaze and his jaw clenched. What right did he have to react in such a way? While he was all too familiar with a young widow who would gladly invite him to her bed, and she was left wound up and still desiring a man who had broken and betrayed her.

Everyone lined up to await their turn. Lady Ockham randomly assigned colors to the turn order. Nick and Lady Preston would take their turn after she and Lord Irvine took theirs, so they lined up beside them.

The heat and electricity she hadn't felt for Lord Irvine hit her like a boulder when Nick came to stand on her other side. She angled herself away from him, facing herself more towards her partner, hoping Nick wouldn't notice her flushed skin. And to keep herself from grabbing Nick and pulling him against her, which was something that she just could not do.

Once the game began, the location of their balls at the end of each turn helped to put a bit of distance between her and Nick, which she was thankful for. Eliza tried to focus on light conversation with her partner. She learnt more about his country home and his beloved horse. She told him of some of her favorite books and he laughed when she confessed how she loathed embroidery. A hatred that she and Juliet had bonded over.

The conversation helped distract her from watching Nick. She found she enjoyed chatting with Lord Irvine, even if she didn't have the urge to bed him. Perhaps the urge would build as she spent more time with him. Her needs certainly weren't going anywhere.

The game progressed with Eliza and Lord Irvine edging out Nick and Lady Preston for the win. Eliza clasped her hands at her chest, cheering their victory.

"What do you say, my lady? How about a kiss for the winner?" Lord Irvine asked.

She stepped closer to him and placed a quick kiss on his cheek, far closer to the corner of his lips than was proper. Let Nick stew over that. "I'd say you earned it," she said, smiling up at him through her lashes.

Lady Ockham approached them with a bundle of flowers and a bottle of brandy. "For the winners," she said, handing Eliza the bouquet and Lord Irvine the bottle.

"Perhaps we might share some of this one evening," Lord Irvine said, holding the bottle up to Eliza.

She glanced at Nick, who had his hands fisted at his sides and his jaw set in a firm line as he observed the scene.

"I would enjoy that very much," she replied to Lord Irvine. Looking back at Nick, she smirked at him. She wasn't yet certain she would encourage a physical arrangement with Lord Irvine, but at least Nick would know that she could do so if she wished. And there wasn't a damn thing he could do about it.

"I would like to put these in my chamber," Eliza said, nodding towards her flowers. "I shall join the others on the terrace after a brief respite." In truth, she just wanted to get away from Nick.

She moved across the grass and climbed the steps to the terrace to reenter the house. She neared the staircase, when suddenly someone grabbed her by her arm. Looking up, she saw Nick's stern expression as he pulled her into the nearest room. He closed the door behind them and locked it.

"What do you think you are doing?" he asked.

She rolled her eyes. "I'm not certain what you mean, nor am I aware what business it is of yours."

He stepped closer to her, and she raised her chin, unwilling to give him the satisfaction of moving away from him.

"You know exactly what I refer to. I won't allow Irvine to dally with you."

She shrugged her shoulders and glanced at the bouquet in her hand. "You would certainly know about dallying."

He released a low growl. "I mean it."

"So do I. And what exactly do you think you are going to do about it?" she asked, stepping so close to him that their chests almost touched, holding the flowers to the side. His familiar, intoxicating scent drove her to distraction. Her thoughts muddled in her head and dampness coated her thighs.

He circled her waist with his arms and pulled her against him. She dropped the flowers to the floor and wrapped her arms around his neck just as he pressed his lips against hers in a searing kiss. She opened for him, and his tongue swept into her mouth. His hands massaged her back and held her tight against him, then she undulated her body hard against his groin, driven wild by the hard bulge in his breeches that pressed against her.

He groaned and gripped the fabric of her skirts, raising them so he could dive his hand between her legs. She moaned against his mouth when his fingers teased her slit.

"So wet," he said. "Is that for him or me?"

Her eyes rolled back in her head when he massaged her pearl, coating it with the wetness from her folds. Her traitorous body wanted everything he could give her. And as much as she'd like to believe herself a more strong-minded woman, she didn't have the willpower to resist.

"Answer me, Eliza," he whispered, his breathing ragged and rough against her ear.

She shook her head, unwilling to admit to him that it was all for him.

He laughed before licking and kissing her neck. "Well, if you wish for me to make you come, you must say so," he said, kissing along her collarbone and stilling the hand that had been teasing her mons.

"Nick," she moaned.

"Yes, Eliza?" He brushed his thumb a single time against her nub. "Was there something you wanted?"

She tightened her hold on him. "Touch me," she pleaded. "Fuck me with your fingers."

"Who do you wish to make come undone, Eliza?" he ground out.

"You," she whispered. "Only you." She should have regretted that she allowed herself to make such an admission, but she lost her good sense with his hand between her thighs.

Nick released a low growl and took her lips again. He edged her back until she was pressed against a nearby wall. He clasped her hands and pinned them to the wall over her head, holding them in place with a single hand. Then he used his free hand to raise her skirts again and resume the attention where she throbbed for him.

She cried out when he slid two fingers inside of her.

"As much as I love to hear you moan, you must be quiet," he said, pressing his lips against hers again.

He increased his pace with his fingers, and she hooked her leg around his hip, causing him to groan into their kiss. When his thumb brushed her pearl, she moaned, and he massaged her tongue harder with his.

With only a few more thrusts of his fingers, she shook and rocked her body against him to draw out her climax for as long as she could, suckling his tongue to keep from crying out.

When she stilled and set her foot back down on the floor, he withdrew his hand and brought his fingers covered in her climax to her lips, then ran the tips of his fingers along her bottom lip before he brought them to his own mouth, sucking and licking them clean. Never once did his eyes leave hers.

She poked her tongue out and licked the wetness from her bottom lip, and then he took her lips again, their tongues mating when she parted her lips to allow him entrance, tasting herself on his tongue.

He released her hands from above her head and shifted back to capture her gaze again. He appeared to contemplate her, and she would have given anything to know what he was thinking. But she was far too proud to ask.

"I think we should discuss what occurred between us," he said.

"Just now?" she asked, scoffing. "I'm uncertain what there is to discuss. Surely you don't require words of gratitude." If he intended to make her feel bad for taking the pleasure he freely offered her, he would find himself disappointed. If he were going to afford her the opportunity, she would take it, and that was that.

He took a small step back. "No, Eliza," he said. "We should discuss what happened three years ago."

She rolled her eyes. "I don't wish to discuss that," she said, brushing down her skirts. "The past is in the past. This changes nothing."

She stepped around him and picked up the bouquet from the floor.

"Eliza, please."

"I achieved an orgasm, so you have served your purpose," she spat, although she knew she wanted so much more from him. "I don't wish to hear a hollow apology from you."

His jaw dropped as if she had struck him. "Why on earth should I apologize to you?" he asked.

She scoffed and hated herself for the tears that instantly formed in her eyes. The man was even more cruel that she believed him capable, and she already knew he was one of the worst men who had ever walked the earth. "You cannot be serious," she said. "You are nothing but a wretched bounder."

Eliza dashed away before he could stop her, unlocking the door and quickly getting herself on the other side of it. She hurried up the stairs, doing her best to keep from drawing notice and feeling grateful as she settled herself on the other side of her chamber door. She must find a way to evict Nicholas Craven from all of her desires, and her heart.

Chapter 6

Nick had finally quelled his anger from earlier that afternoon. Well, perhaps not completely, but his breathing had at least returned to normal. How dare she demand an apology from him? He still didn't understand why his father told him she had married when she hadn't, but he reasoned his father had only the best of intentions. Nick had been miserable for several months while he licked his wounds from Eliza's rejection. He surmised that his father merely took pity on him and wished to help his son mend his broken heart.

It hadn't mended very well, since the mere presence of the vexing woman tore the wounds wide open, leaving his heart laid bare. If she thought he would stand by and allow her to throw herself at Lord Irvine right in front of him, she was indeed mistaken. He would make her explain herself, so he might be able to finally put her, and what they shared, in the past.

She at least owed him that, to put him out of his misery by divulging the reasons she had for abandoning him. Even if a part of him, a larger one that he cared to admit, still loved her, he couldn't build a life with someone who would treat him so callously and walk away from the depths of the love he'd believed they had shared, and then throw herself at other men.

He glanced around the salon. And he wouldn't bother to lie to himself and pretend he wasn't looking for her. Before the house party had concluded, he would learn why she wouldn't see him to explain why she lied about loving him. About her being his. When he pulled her aside earlier, he hadn't expected to lose all of his self-control. Something primal in him took over when her lips touched Irvine's cheek, and he needed to possess her.

She was supposed to always be his. A fact she seemed to have forgotten, or perhaps it was a tribute to her incredible acting abilities. He downed the rest of his brandy and continued watching for her.

Ockham approached him as Nick refilled his glass.

"Are you enjoying yourself?" Ockham asked.

"Indeed," Nick replied, holding up his glass. It would be a regular lie as long as he was trapped in the same house with Eliza, reliving the best memories and worst pains of his life.

"My wife would be quite put out if you weren't, so I am glad to hear it."

Nick shook his head and laughed. "We can't have that. I might be just a tad afraid of her, if we are honest."

"Me too, my good man," Ockham jested. "But she's the best thing that ever happened to me."

Nick fought the urge to gag and sought to change the subject. "It seems that Rosina might have found someone who caught her eye," Nick said, nodding towards where Lady Rosina Preston stood chatting with the Duke of St. Albans.

"I thought you might have taken an interest since you partnered with her for Pall Mall," Ockham said, assessing his reaction.

Laughing, Nick elbowed his friend. "I'd never take our dear friend's widow to bed. God rest his soul. I wonder what he'd think of her resolve to remain unwed, and well...you know."

"Well, my wife finds the lady's intentions admirable and supports a woman's decision to decide her own future. She's probably right. Who are we to judge what the lady wishes to do?" Ockham asked, shrugging. "Besides, my wife and I had bets on who the lady would select, and it appears my wife just might win."

Nick eyed his friend curiously. "What are the terms of this bet?"

Ockham laughed and patted his friend on the back. "I shan't tell you, but just know that either way, I come out a winner."

Nick rolled his eyes and took a large gulp of his drink. "I'm sure you do." He glanced around the room again and tamped down his irritation that Eliza hadn't made her appearance yet. A sudden panic overtook him, and he scanned the room, looking for Lord Irvine. Every second he spent trying to locate the man constricted his chest tighter.

Finally, he spotted him in the corner chatting with a few other guests, Eliza not in his company, either. The tension eased slightly.

"My wife also has some ideas on who you might pair nicely with, Craven."

Eye rolls were going to be common for the duration of the house party as well, it would seem. "I have already told you that I'm not interested."

"Are you ever going to tell me who the woman was?" Ockham asked. "Surely enough time has passed that you might be ready to move on."

"If your wife had rejected you to marry another, would your heart so easily recover?" Nick asked, then felt bad for snapping at his friend. Even if Nick knew she hadn't actually married, his friend wasn't aware of that new revelation, and better to keep to the story. At least they wouldn't be able to guess who the mystery lady was. His hosts would become tiresome if they knew his past love was in attendance at their party.

The man frowned, and his eyes pained in response. "No, it wouldn't. Please accept my apologies."

"None needed," Nick said. "Don't worry about me. I am perfectly well."

Ockham's wife approached, and both gentlemen shifted their attention to her, bowing.

"Everything all right, my love?" Ockham asked.

She looped her arm in her husband's and laid her free hand on the same bicep. Nick hated how his heart pained at the simple gesture between the couple.

"Indeed. Lady Eliza isn't feeling well, so I had a tray and tisane sent to her chamber."

Nick took a large gulp of his drink to keep from asking his hostess questions about Eliza. He had little doubt that Eliza only feigned illness to avoid seeing him after their encounter that afternoon. She couldn't hide from him for the entire party. He would get the answers he needed from her. She at least owed him that.

A pretty, voluptuous miss approached their group. Nick recognized her as the friend that had been at Eliza's side last night and at breakfast. She curtsied to the group and spoke to their hostess. "Do I have enough time to check on Eliza before dinner?" she asked. "I just wish to see that she is all right."

Lady Ockham eyed the clock on the mantel. "I should think so. Dinner shall be served in another quarter hour." Lady Ockham glanced at Nick. "Lady Juliet, have you been introduced to Lord Craven?"

Nick saw a flash of shock and then anger cross the young lady's expression before settling on a tight smile. Interesting. She must have some awareness of his and Eliza's past. He wasn't sure why it delighted him that Eliza had spoken of him to another, even though it appeared that the young lady didn't think too highly of him.

"I don't believe we have," Nick said, bowing to her. "Pleased to meet you, my lady."

She attempted to widen her smile, but it didn't reach her eyes. "You as well, my lord," she replied. "If you all will excuse me, I shall return in a moment."

Lady Juliet turned on her heel and departed the salon.

Nick noted Onslow near the exit and took his opportunity. "I need to speak with Onslow about something, if you could excuse me as well," Nick said. He didn't wait for them to respond and crossed the room to Onslow.

Nick looked back to see if his hosts were watching him, but they had been approached by another couple. He bypassed Onslow and hurried to the staircase, then darted up the stairs, hoping to see which room Lady Juliet would enter. He took a left off of the staircase and saw a shadow down the hallway. Nick quickened his pace and caught sight of a door clicking closed. He crept to the door and put his ear to it.

He should be ashamed of himself for eavesdropping, but he was desperate to get to the bottom of what had occurred between them. If he could overhear something useful, he could forgive himself for using devious means to obtain the information.

"Why didn't you tell me he was here?" Lady Juliet asked. "Is he the reason you are hiding in your chamber?"

"I planned to tell you. Today, in fact. I promise," Eliza said. "I just didn't know what to think about seeing him again. I still don't."

"So he was the reason for your poor mood this morning."

"No," Eliza said, then paused for a few seconds, which felt like hours to Nick. "Well, all right. Yes. His presence is quite distracting."

"He really is quite handsome. I can see how he would set your head to a spin and why you took him to your bed," Lady Juliet said.

Nick grinned to himself with his ear still pressed against the door. He found it interesting, indeed, that Eliza had told her friend about the two of them being intimate.

"Jules!"

"Well, it's true," Lady Juliet said. "One does have to wonder why he never took a wife."

"He probably just dallies with whomever he wishes and casts them aside when he is finished," Eliza said.

He balled his hands into fists and fought to keep himself from barging into her room. She was the one who was the expert in dallying with one's affections, and yet she treated him as the villain.

"He's certainly riled you up. Have you given more thought to making good use of the house party to entertain a tryst?" Lady Juliet asked. "I saw you flirting with Lord Irvine. And don't try to convince me otherwise."

Nick pressed his ear harder against the door, not daring to miss Eliza's response. He tamped down the mixture of jealousy, hurt, and fury bubbling far too close to the surface.

"I'm considering it," Eliza said. "I'm still not certain. But I shall have ample opportunity to decide. I certainly believe he would be amenable. He can't keep his eyes off my chest."

He heard laughter coming from both of the ladies, when he found nothing humorous about the mere suggestion that Eliza would take up with another man in the ways that he had been with her. She had been passionate and an active participant in their couplings, extremely vocal as well, and he didn't want anyone else to experience that side of her. Especially not where he would be far too aware of what had occurred.

"I must return downstairs to join the party for dinner," Lady Juliet said after the laughter subsided. "I will visit again when I retire for the evening."

Nick hurried away from the door and darted back downstairs, hoping that he had enough of a head start that Eliza's friend wouldn't see him making his escape.

He made it back to the salon several seconds before Juliet re-entered the party. Nick hadn't considered that if anyone had seen them, they might believe that it was Juliet he had snuck from the room to meet.

Attempting to prevent anyone from getting such ideas, he joined a group of gentlemen near the sideboard.

"Irvine might have a chance with Lady Eliza," Lord Duncan said.

Nick fought to school his features. She was everywhere, even when she wasn't in the room, she was still there taunting him and driving him to distraction.

"But I didn't think he wished to wed. At least not anytime soon." Lord Onslow replied.

Lord Duncan laughed before taking a swig from the drink in his hand. "I didn't say anything about marriage."

Nick fisted his hands, contemplating planting the man a facer and then marching over to Irvine and giving him one in each eye.

Before he did just that, the dinner bell rang. He wasn't certain how he was going to get through the rest of the evening if Eliza continued to be the topic of conversation.

Nick tossed and turned in his bed. His body and mind were at war with themselves. His cock stood at attention when he recalled the taste of Eliza's climax on his fingers, a sweet nectar he had missed more than he'd allowed himself to admit, longed for even. But his head replayed the ladies' conversation and Eliza's contemplation with that rake, Lord Irvine. He was at least thankful that he went the rest of the evening without one of the gentlemen bringing up Eliza again. Thank God for small favors.

When the sun emerged from the horizon that next morning, he gave up on the notion of restful sleep.

Climbing out of the bed, he wrapped his banyan around himself before washing his face with the cool water in the washbasin.

He glanced down and his cock protruded in front of him and refused to relent, aching from the intensity of the thoughts that invaded his sleep. He willed it to subside, not wanting to think of the one person he wished would ease his need. Trying not to think of her only made him think of her more. Made him want her more.

Nick couldn't have his valet help to dress him in such a state, his member fully erect and throbbing. He tried to think of something else, but his mind kept coming back to her. It always came back to her.

Where he stood, he fisted himself and stroked up and down his shaft. He let his head fall back and stiffened his legs, stroking and teasing the steel rod between his legs as he imagined her lips wrapped around his cock. He thrust his hips to meet his hand, increasing his speed, still imagining her tongue stroking the smooth underside. She used to love when he fucked her mouth, leaving him with a wet surprise he could lap up between her thighs.

Before he came, he grabbed a cloth from the washstand and whispered her name when he released himself into the soft fabric.

He set the soiled cloth on the table and tied his banyan closed. He was still half erect, his need only momentarily sated, but perhaps he might better have his wits about him. Thinking about Eliza wouldn't help, but he must get her alone so he could ask her why she abandoned him. Why she told him she loved him and would always be his, only to disappear and refuse to see him.

And more importantly, he'd have to ensure that a rake-hell like Lord Irvine didn't put his hands on her.

Chapter 7

E liza and Juliet strolled into the breakfast room, arm in arm again. Eliza wasn't ready to face Nick after what had transpired between them, but she knew Juliet wouldn't fall for any attempts to delay their arrival in the breakfast room. She didn't care to admit to herself how much the man still affected her. Her body craved him and her heart longed for him. But he was merely toying with her affections, and she was the fool for turning wanton in his presence. What made the matter ironic was that he was the one who had unlocked her wanton desires, and he still wielded the power to engage them at his will.

It wouldn't be a surprise when he tossed her aside at the conclusion of the house party. Given his attention to Lady Preston, he probably had multiple women at his disposal.

He dallied with her because he knew he could, and she had willingly allowed him to do so.

The odious man didn't even believe he owed her an apology for tricking her, breaking her heart, and, in fact, ruining her. Her choices for a husband were limited—not that she wished to take one. She may have had many proposals, but once they knew another man had already taken her maidenhead, they would cast her aside. They could even seek an annulment or treat her poorly.

Worse than that, even after three years, she hadn't dislodged him from her thoughts, and—she hated to admit—her heart. If yesterday had been any indication, her body betrayed her in how much she wanted him.

"Good morning, ladies," Lord Irvine said, bowing to them. "Allow me to help you to your seats."

They each took one of his proffered arms and when she glanced up at the man, it wasn't lost on her that his gaze had locked onto her chest again. She glanced at Juliet, who smirked and stifled a giggle.

"Are you feeling all right this morning, Lady Eliza?" he asked. "I was disappointed when you didn't join the rest of us for dinner."

She caught sight of Nick entering the breakfast room, and her breath caught. She instantly pushed the notion aside and reminded herself that no good could come from thinking of him as anything but the horrid man who used her and cast her aside.

"I am feeling much better, indeed," she said, smiling up through her lashes. She bit her bottom lip for good measure and almost laughed when the man's gaze immediately fixed there. Men really were simple creatures.

Eliza still wasn't certain that she wished to couple with Lord Irvine, but it appeared the option would be available for her if she chose to pursue it. He may be a rake, but he had been kind and attentive to her, at least. He was likely a skilled bed partner, too, if she allowed herself to consider it.

He escorted them to the sideboard, where they made their selections. He carried each of their plates to the table and set them down, then pulled out their chairs and seated each of the ladies. Lord Irvine seated himself in the open seat next to Eliza, positioning his chair closer to her than he ought. When he sat down, his thigh rubbed against hers.

She noted that there still wasn't even a hint of excitement or anticipation at having him so close. When she had been anywhere near Nick, or any part of them barely touched, the electricity had been palpable. It drew them closer together so that they sought any excuse to touch each other. Which was still evident based on what had occurred between them the day before.

She mentally chastised herself for comparing her reaction to anything regarding Nick. What she and Nick had wasn't real. At least not for him. He made that quite clear. So perhaps she couldn't be trusted to know what attraction or connection was. And did it truly even matter if all she would ask of Lord Irvine was physical pleasure? It's not like she would ever consider marrying the man. She didn't need him to cuddle her and whisper sweet nothings.

She opened her mouth to speak to Lord Irvine and closed it again when Nick took the seat directly across from her. Refusing to look at him, she refocused her attention on the man beside her, even if her body betrayed her attraction to Nick. "I hear a group is going to go riding after breakfast. I hoped you might accompany me, my lord."

"I would be honored to ride with you, my lady," Lord Irvine replied. "Do you enjoy horseback riding?"

"I do very much," she said, looking up from her plate to offer him a wide smile. She glanced at Nick, whose neck had turned red, and his gaze bored into her. She rolled her eyes at him and took another bite of her food. Eliza glanced at Juliet and noted that Marquess Theodore Camden had seated himself next to her and had her engaged in conversation.

With her friend distracted, she focused her attention back on Lord Irvine. She tried to think of something to speak to him about, but Nick beat her to it.

"Will you be entering a horse in Newmarket next season, Irvine?" Nick asked.

"I intend to. I recently bought a fine contender from the Clive family, and I believe he shall be up to scratch," Lord Irvine replied. John Clive was the most sought-after horse breeder in England since he took over the business from his cousin, who had unexpectedly become a titled peer.

Eliza masked her irritation at Nick's interference and focused her attention on her plate. She tuned out the monotonous conversation about horses and races while picking at her food. She suspected Nick might have engaged the man in conversation to prevent her from doing so. Why did he care what she did or who she entertained, in her bed or out of it? He'd lost the right to do so.

She didn't speak for the rest of breakfast, all too glad when she could excuse herself to change into her riding habit. She could only hope that she could escape Nick during the group ride, but she had erred when she asked Lord Irvine to accompany her in front of him.

After breakfast, Dot helped her to dress, and once her bonnet was set, she tapped her knuckles on Juliet's door.

"Come in," she heard from the other side of the door.

Eliza entered the room and then closed the door behind her.

"I shall be ready in a few moments," Juliet said, seated at the vanity where her maid was adjusting her hair.

"I'm certain they won't depart without us, and if they do, we shall go riding on our own," Eliza said, taking a seat in a nearby chair.

"Perhaps you hope to avoid a certain gentleman," Juliet returned, catching her friend's eye in the mirror.

Eliza rolled her eyes. "You must have missed where I asked Lord Irvine to accompany me."

"What I didn't miss is how you are still attracted to Lord Craven," Juliet returned. "Not that I blame you, of course."

"Have you forgotten how the man treated me?" Eliza asked. "He made me believe he loved me and wished to marry me, then used a coward's letter to inform me that it was all a cruel trick."

Juliet waved off her words. "Of course not. But your eyes don't lie. And neither do his. There is certainly something between the two of you."

"You know not of what you speak of, Juliet," Eliza said, tamping down her irritation. "He is merely dallying with me and taunting me for being so foolish."

"And just how is he dallying with you?" Juliet asked, casting her a knowing look.

Eliza's cheeks pinkened. "I might have allowed him to touch me a bit."

"Might have? You know I want details."

"All right, I did. Just a bit of kissing, and his hands ventured between my legs." And it was far better than any of the climaxes she had been reduced to giving herself.

Juliet clasped her hands together. "I knew it. I knew there was something between you still. You are trying so hard to fight it."

Eliza shook her head. "I just wanted him to make me come. Nothing more. He only did so because he wished to dally with me, so I took the opportunity to ensure my own needs were met. He has done so, and that is that."

Juliet shook her head. "I think there is more to it."

"What of you?" Eliza asked, attempting to shift the conversation. "You seemed to find Lord Camden to be interesting company. You hardly spoke to me at breakfast."

Her friend tried to mask the pink of her cheeks, but her reaction wasn't so easily hidden from Eliza.

"He is interesting for certain." Juliet's riding bonnet was set and tied, and she rose from her stool. "I am ready."

"Let's be off then," Eliza said. Anything to prevent further conversation about Nick. She would spend the day in Lord Irvine's company and perhaps entertain something physical between them. The idea became more appealing if it should help to push Nick from her thoughts.

When they arrived at the stables, the horses were saddled and ready. Her entire body tingled with awareness when Nick stepped close to her to climb atop the horse next to hers. Lord Irvine offered his assistance to help Eliza seat herself in the saddle and then climbed atop his horse.

The ride was relaxing for the most part. With so many others on the outing with them, she forced herself to ignore Nick as best as she could. During the ride, Lady Preston had ridden up next to him and engaged him in conversation.

Eliza had tried to eavesdrop on what they discussed, but Lord Irvine distracted her with questions about her various interests. It prevented her from hearing any of what the lady said to Nick, and it left her irritated. Not that she was jealous. The man was mad to interfere with Eliza's prospects when he was more than likely fucking the very woman in his friend's house, all the while dipping his fingers inside Eliza in one of their host's small parlors.

After riding for a couple of hours, the group stopped for a picnic by a pond. The day was perfect, with the sun high in the partly cloudy skies. The light breeze hit her face and the cool fall air kissed her cheeks. It looked as if it might rain later, but it was still beautiful out.

"Lady Eliza," Lord Irvine said, getting her attention beside her, "I thought we might share a drink of our spirits this evening to toast our win yesterday."

She glanced at him and noticed his dark eyes had a few flecks of gold in them, which shone under the September sun. He was handsome, to be sure. If he ever wished to marry one day, he'd melt hearts.

"I would enjoy that, my lord." There wouldn't be harm in having a drink with the man, and she could see how she might feel about entertaining something more. It would certainly be one way to get Nick out of her head.

After dinner that evening, the house party had retired to the salon for music. The women in attendance took turns singing and playing the pianoforte. Eliza and Juliet paired for a duet, playing the pianoforte together and singing. They had done so a few times before at other parties and had always received a warm reception. When they finished, the group erupted into cheers and applause.

Eliza couldn't help but notice Nick's expression, which appeared to show the faintest signs of remorse. He caught her eye, and the intensity of his gaze sent shivers up her spine.

"My lady," Lord Irvine said, capturing her attention. He held his hand out to her to help her up from the bench. "I thought we might take our drink on the terrace. It's a lovely evening and not too terribly cold." He leaned a bit closer. "And our drink shall keep us warm." He smiled down at her, his expression full of mirth.

She responded by looping her arm in his and allowing him to lead the way. He already held the bottle they had won in the Pall Mall competition, and he stopped before they reached the terrace door to grab two glasses from the sideboard.

Once they were outside on the terrace, he poured them each a drink before he set the bottle down on the wide top rail. "To our win, and what a great team we make," he said, holding his glass up in a toast.

She toasted him, and they each took a large gulp of their drinks. He was right about it keeping her warm as her throat had already warmed as she downed the liquid.

"If I may be so forward," he started after lowering his glass, "why is it you have turned down so many offers of marriage, my lady?"

She took another fortifying sip of her drink before responding. "I don't wish to marry."

"Then we have that in common," he said. "At least for a very long time, indeed."

"I am sure you will take a wife one day to secure your heir, but I never intend to marry." She fell for the folly of schoolgirl notions once, and she would be damned if she'd go through that heartache again.

"But don't you wish for"—he paused and captured her gaze—"other things?"

She smirked at him. "Does one truly need to be married to engage in such things? I would wager you haven't been living as a monk, my lord."

He choked on the sip he took and coughed a few times. Once he recovered, he responded. "I quite enjoy a lady who is so forward."

Perhaps it was the drink or even the moonlight, but she found she enjoyed flirting with the man. Perhaps if she kissed him, she would feel a bit more inclined to allow other liberties and forget Nick once and for all.

"And I enjoy a gentleman who thinks so," she said, giving him a coy grin.

He stepped closer to her and removed her drink from her hand, then set both of their glasses beside the bottle on the railing. "Lady Eliza, might you be amenable to a kiss?"

"I believe I would, my lord," she said, smiling up at him. She wasn't certain, but it was time. Time to see what another man might stir within her. She had only ever kissed Nick, and if one would have asked her three years ago, she would have said she would kiss no other man for as long as she lived. But unless she wished to never experience the touch of a man again, she had to try.

He cupped her face in his hand and glanced at her lips. Much to her annoyance, she pictured Nick's face and longed for the man before her to be him.

"Irvine," a familiar voice called out as if she had conjured Nick from her thoughts. "Our hosts have requested your presence."

Lord Irvine quickly dropped his hand and stepped back from Eliza.

"Of course," he said before turning back to Eliza, whispering so only she could hear. "I should like to continue this later."

She nodded and watched him depart before pushing past Nick to return inside. Eliza was afraid of what she might do or say to him if she remained in his presence, wanting him as much as she did. She didn't trust herself not to drag him to her bed. So she took off through the other doorway and down a corridor to avoid being seen by the other guests.

But she hadn't been fast enough as Nick was quickly on her heels. His firm hand grabbed her arm and pulled her into a small study with only a few bookcases and a desk. There was a bit of light in the room from the low embers glowing from the fireplace.

Nick closed the door behind them and leaned against it. The shadows on his face made him appear a tad dangerous, yet irresistibly handsome. "Eliza," he said, breathless and frenzied. His nostrils flared and his jaw set in a hard line. "What in the hell do you think you are doing?"

Chapter 8

Nick fought to keep his hurt and anger under control. If he had arrived even a few seconds later, she would have been in the man's arms and his lips would have been upon hers. That was something he just could not allow. The man would be confused when their hosts did not know why Irvine sought them out, but it was the first thing Nick could come up with to get the man to leave.

"Last I checked," she started, "if I wish to fuck a handsome gentleman, I am free to do so."

His blood boiled, and he stepped closer to her. "No, you aren't," he ground out. She was right, of course, but she should have married him. She was always supposed to be his, and even with all that had happened between them, and all that he still didn't understand, he still wanted her. That much he knew for certain. His body, his cock…his heart, his soul…all wanted her.

She closed the distance between them, stopping just out of his reach. "From what I hear, he is quite well known for his prowess. I'm sure he'll be able to satisfy me in bed. Perhaps he'll even teach me a few things."

He released a low growl and stepped closer so he could pull her to him. "I will not allow you to fuck Irvine. Or any other man." He bent his head to kiss her collarbone and neck, causing her to sway in his arms. At least he still affected her.

She didn't pull away and instead matched his dare by licking along his jaw until she reached his ear. "It is no business of yours if I should wish to come all over his thick cock," she whispered.

He didn't believe she actually knew the girth of Irvine's manhood. But her words still grated on Nick's nerves.

"Perhaps you should bend over that desk so I can remind you who you belong to, Eliza," he said, running his hands down her back and clasping her bottom, pulling her against his rock-hard erection.

Releasing a low mewl, she placed her hands on his chest, pushing him slightly back. "Perhaps you should drop to your knees and do something more useful with your tongue."

She was going to be the death of him. But if she intended that as a challenge, he wouldn't back down. He pressed his lips to hers and she swept her tongue into his mouth, taking control of the kiss. He moved her backwards until she was backed against the furniture. When her bottom was pressed against the side of the large oak desk, he broke the kiss.

"Lift your skirts," he commanded.

She did as he said, and her beautiful slit was bare before him within a nest of dark curls. He licked his lips and dropped to his knees. When he ran his tongue along her pearl, she leaned her bottom against the desk and released a stream of moans. He sucked her nub, and she clasped his head in her hands.

It wasn't enough. He needed to show her what she'd missed. What she could have had every single day for the last three years if she hadn't given up on them.

He pulled away and looked up at her. "Bend over the desk," he said.

"After that lackluster performance?" she asked, smirking at him.

He released a low growl. "Bend over the desk, and I'll remind you exactly what my tongue can do." He rose and pressed his lips to hers, running his tongue just inside her lips so she could taste herself. Shifting to her jaw, he kissed and licked until he reached her ear and whispered, "I would wager your arse has missed me, too."

She looked for a mere moment as if she might hold her resolve, but desire made her eyelids heavy and her chest rose with the intensity of her breath. He knew her body and her wants well enough to know that his words would be her undoing. She turned around and did as he said, leaning low over the desk, bracing herself on her arms. He positioned himself on his knees between her legs and lifted her skirts again so that her bottom was fully exposed to him. He urged her to widen her stance and then clasped the cheeks of her bottom in each of his hands.

Spreading her open, he buried his face in her. He licked from her nub to her wet core, plunging his tongue inside of her. She rocked and moaned over the desk. He continued his exploration and ran his tongue up past her heat to the tight, puckered hole of her arse.

"Yes, Nick," she moaned.

He licked and teased her arse with his tongue, while dipping two fingers inside of her dripping wet heat. Nick pulled back, entranced with everything about her, knowing it was him who caused her folds to glisten from her arousal. He removed his fingers from inside of her and traced them around the hole of her arse, applying the wetness to ease his inevitable invasion. He inserted a single finger just to the first knuckle, and she moaned, laying herself flat on top of the desk and pushing herself back into him.

Nick had her where he wanted her. He knew every inch of her body and what she needed. Better than anyone, he knew how to give it to her. He would remind her why she never should have left him. That there was no other man alive who could please her the way he did. And as much as he hated to admit it, he just might destroy any man who tried.

He slid his finger further into her arse, reaching the next knuckle.

"Fuck, yes," she whimpered. "Don't stop."

He grinned and licked his lips, glad to see she hadn't lost the foul mouth she picked up from the wicked nights they had spent together.

"If I had oil, I'd give you the full length of my cock," he teased, pulling his finger out and sliding it back in to the same knuckle.

She whimpered and pushed back against him, taking more of his finger. He leaned forward again and returned his attention to her pearl, massaging it with his tongue while she bucked and rode his face and finger. Her arse was so tight on his finger, his cock threatened to rip a hole in his breeches.

Eliza cried out into her hand and shook when she came, and he lapped up every drop of her climax until she stilled. He stood and took in the sight of her. She was perfect. Lying with her arse bare before him, her core glistening, and her pearl swollen. Her cheek was pressed against the desk while she caught her breath, and her skin was flushed. Her stockings were up to her thighs, and he massaged the exposed fleshy area.

He leaned into her, pressing his covered bulge against her naked bottom. "Now you must tell me what you want."

She pushed her bottom harder against his bulge and he closed his eyes, sucking in a deep breath. She was begging to be fucked, and he recalled how another man might have attempted to do so that very evening. His heart ached with how much he still loved her.

"I'm still unclear who you believe I belong to," she said, moving her bottom to rub against him.

"If you don't know by now, what do you expect me to do about it?" he asked, thrusting his hard ridge against her. He knew exactly what she wanted, but he would make her say it. He needed to remind her of why she had no need to seek out another man. She had never needed anyone else and shouldn't have abandoned him. She had been everything to him, and he would have spent every minute of his life ensuring he was everything to her.

"Bury your cock deep inside of me and don't go slow," she said.

He fumbled with his falls, releasing himself so he could do just as she commanded. Once his member sprang free, he stroked it a few times in his hand, teasing the opening of her wet cunt with the head of his cock. He sucked in a breath at how good her delicate, wet skin felt against his.

"And just whose cock is that you want?" he asked, running a hand along her hip, giving it a squeeze.

"Nick," she groaned, pleading with him. "I want you now."

He slid himself inside of her and thrust hard, gripping her hips. It was like coming home. With every thrust, his heart pounded, believing that perhaps if he fucked her hard enough, loved her hard enough, she might regret tossing aside what they had together.

But a troubling thought crossed his mind.

"Have you been with anyone else?" he asked, not slowing his movements, keeping the pace she commanded.

She moaned and pushed against him, driving him deeper inside of her. "Why should you care?" she said between each of his thrusts.

"Just tell me now," he said through gritted teeth, punishing her with each thrust. "I shall issue a challenge to anyone who touched you."

"Don't stop," she panted. "That is so fucking good."

He continued holding one of her hips and slid his other hand to rest on her back, holding her in place against the desk when he thrust harder. "Answer me, Eliza," he said through labored breaths.

"No one, Nick," she panted. "Only you."

He turned feral, the intensity of his thrusts claiming her. She was still his. There had to be a reason she hadn't been with anyone else, or accepted any of the proposals she received. Fool as he was, hope crept in that perhaps he could win her heart. That he would learn why she abandoned him and ensure she never did so again.

Clenching hard around his cock, she covered her mouth when she reached the pinnacle of her pleasure, rocking hard against him. He withdrew just in time and moaned her name in a low whisper as he stroked himself to claim every bit of his well earned climax, his seed shooting across her bottom.

He pulled his handkerchief from his pocket and gently wiped between her legs before wiping away the evidence of the most exquisite experience he'd had since he'd been with her over three years ago.

Nick tenderly kissed the flesh of one of her supple arse cheeks before he pulled her skirts down. He helped her to stand, then tucked himself back into his falls. He placed a light kiss on her lips before pulling away and staring into her eyes. Aching for answers to all of his questions.

"Why, Eliza?" he finally asked. "Why do you hate me so?"

Confusion and hurt marred her beautiful face before she released an angry laugh. "Are you quite serious?"

"I find nothing humorous about it," he replied. "I thought you loved me."

"Have you gone mad?" she asked.

He released her and dropped his arms. Perhaps she was just as heartless as he had believed her to be for the past few years. He had been nothing more than a fool to allow himself to hope otherwise. "So you never loved me then?"

"Why are you being so cruel?" she asked. "Do you wish for me to say the words so you can reject me again?"

He ran his fingers through his hair. How dare she? "Reject you?" he scoffed. "Reject you? Now who has gone mad?"

She poked her finger at his chest. "You are the one who is mad. I waited at the hunting cabin all night for you and the next day you told me you never loved me with a letter. A letter. My love for you was so intense and true that I would have sold my soul to the devil himself to be your wife, to have you inside me every night, to be the one you loved and cherished. Is that what you wish to hear?"

His stomach reeled, and he fought to keep his balance. "What letter?"

Eliza stepped around him. "I can't believe you." She released an exasperated groan and flailed her hands in the air. "This is done. Play your games with someone else. You're still a great fuck, but I am done being sucked back into your web of deceit and playing your fool."

She raced from the room before he could stop her. He gripped the side of the desk. Letter? What letter? He never sent a letter. *Hell and damnation.* He closed his eyes, fighting to keep himself from losing control. He fisted his hands and slammed one down onto the desk.

Someone tore them apart. That was the only thing that could possibly make any sense. Undoubtedly, their fathers. *Goddamn them.* What a fool he had been, playing right into their deceit.

He left the small study and noticed that the house was quiet. The other guests must have retired to their rooms for the evening. The lack of movement in the household would prove to be beneficial so he could speak to Eliza again. It couldn't wait. He needed to know what letter she spoke of so they might ascertain what evil scheme their fathers had played on them both, robbing them of their lifetime of happiness together.

He crept up the stairs and made his way down the hallway as quietly as he could until he reached her door. Trying the knob, he was thankful to find it unlocked, and stepped inside, closing and locking the door behind him.

From the light of the fire crackling in the fireplace and the single candle lit on the bedside table, he saw Eliza sprawled across her bed. Her shoulders were shaking as she sobbed into her pillow. It had been there the whole time if he would have allowed himself to consider the pain she carried. If he had only known. His heart ached and tears welled in his eyes, realizing she had hurt as much as he had in their years apart.

"Eliza," he whispered.

Chapter 9

Eliza didn't pick her head up when she heard Nick's voice. The pain was far too great to face him again. She deserved to feel the depth of her suffering in peace and not to have him bear witness. "Go away," she cried into her pillow. "Please." The last word came out as a sob.

He didn't do as she asked and stepped closer, kneeling on the floor beside her head. "My love, I never sent you a letter." His voice cracked on the last few words.

"What?" she asked, lifting her head to look at him. "You did. Why are you doing this?"

He shook head, agony written on his features. "I didn't."

She climbed off the bed and dug around in her trunk until she returned with the crumpled piece of parchment, the one she had read thousands of times, which would remind him of the pain and destruction he had caused since he seemed to have forgotten. She shoved it into his hands.

He stood and unfolded the paper, holding it closer to the candle. She watched his pained expression and slumped shoulders as he read the missive. "I didn't write this, Eliza. Where did you get this?"

"My father gave it…" her voice trailed off before the realization washed over her face. "I can't believe this." She shook, and a heart-wrenching sob escaped her body. How could their fathers have done this to her? To them?

Nick rushed to her and wrapped his arms around her. "I never stopped loving you, sweetheart, I promise."

"I…I don't know what to think."

He eyed the missive again. "You have carried this with you for three years?"

She sighed and tears streamed down her cheeks. "I needed it to remind me why I was foolish to love you and why I could never give my heart to another." Eliza had taken it with her everywhere she went and read it more times than she would ever admit. Part of her carried it with her because it was all she had from him and the only reminder that what they had shared had really happened.

Nick embraced her again. "I have always loved you, Eliza."

She pushed back from him. The whole situation still made little sense. "Why didn't you come for me? Why didn't you meet me at the hunting cabin?"

"I came to call on you earlier that day for tea. I couldn't wait until that evening to see you," he said, reaching out to take her hand in his. "Your butler told me you had left for London."

"So you just gave up and never tried to see me again? You just walked away?" she asked, trying to pull her hand from his, but he gripped it tighter.

"I left for town a quarter hour after I heard you had left. I hoped to catch up with you on the road, to no avail. Then, when I finally arrived, I went straight to your family's townhouse. Your butler there said you didn't wish to see me."

She sat on the edge of the bed, and he sat beside her. Her father had their servants in on his deception. Servants she would have believed she could trust. "I can't believe this."

"I went back to your townhouse every day for weeks, begging your butler to have you see me. I tried to break into your house but was caught and thrown out. I left notes for you and I sent you flowers. At the start of the season, I went to every event and searched for you in every ballroom, hoping to find you there to make you speak with me."

"I didn't go to Town for the season," she said, sighing. "I delayed my come out a year because I was too miserable and heartbroken to attend society events. I just stayed in my room and missed you. Hating and chastising myself for missing someone who I believed never loved me."

She couldn't control her sobs, and he pulled her close, rubbing her back as her shoulders shook. "If my father weren't already dead, I might kill him," he said.

"Why your father?" she asked, wiping her eyes with her hand. "My father must have done this. He had our entire household in on the deception. I can't believe he would break his own daughter's heart over something as frivolous as a stream." She couldn't imagine hatred and bad blood being so strong to ruin your own flesh and blood.

"I don't believe he acted alone," Nick said. "That letter you received is in my father's hand. The only reason I stopped trying to find you is because my father told me after a couple months of my endless search for you that you had married. I didn't even ask to whom. Ockham was in Italy, so with a broken heart, I left the next day so I wouldn't risk seeing you with your husband."

She touched his cheek, realizing how hurt they had both been these last few years. "When you saw me here, you asked where my husband was. I thought you were being cruel and mocked how I believed you would marry me," she said. "I'm sorry I said such awful things to you."

"Please don't apologize. I will never forgive myself for falling into their trap or for the unforgivable things I also said to you," he said, holding her tight in his arms. "I love you, Eliza. I always have, and I always will."

"I love you, too, Nick." She nuzzled his neck. She had never stopped loving him either, but she just hadn't been willing to admit it to herself. Believing it made her a fool with no self-respect for loving a man who could discard her so easily, but like some sort of Shakespearean tragedy, they both loved and longed for each other every day they had been apart.

He released her and slid off the bed to kneel before her. He took her hands in his and looked up at her, locking on her gaze. "Lady Eliza Nelson, will you please marry me? I will spend every single day of our lives making up for the time we lost and every tear you shed believing my heart didn't ache for you."

"I want nothing more in this world than to be your wife, Lord Nicholas Craven."

He rose and pulled her to him. She needed his kiss the same as she required air in her lungs. She sank into him, and they fit together perfectly, the same as they had from their very first kiss.

"We shall depart tomorrow," he said. "Our hosts will understand once we explain things to them. We can get a special license and marry right away."

"Yes, I don't wish to wait any longer than is required," she said. "It's just…"

"What, my love?" he asked. "What is it?"

She laid her head on his shoulder. "I don't believe I should wish to see my papa again. I don't think I can forgive him for what he did. For whatever part he played in this scheme." How could she be expected to face the man after what he had done to them? She wasn't certain that she or Nick could do so without inflicting bodily harm.

He kissed her forehead. "I'm not certain I will ever forgive him either, but I will support whatever you wish if you should change your mind one day," he said. "You needn't decide now. You are of age, and he can't stop us from marrying. I don't give a fig about your dowry if he withholds it."

"Thank you, my love," she said, releasing a small sigh of relief. There was nothing they could do to change the past, and it was time they focused on their future. They had lost far too much time together already.

"We will send for your things, and we'll buy whatever you require so you don't have to step foot inside your father's home again if you don't wish to."

"Please don't leave me tonight," she pleaded, and if she had her way, she would never sleep apart from him again. "I don't wish to be apart from you. I'm afraid I shall wake up in the middle of the night and find this has all been a dream."

He brought her hand to his lips and kissed her knuckles. "There is nothing in this world that could get me to part from you. I have lost far too many nights of holding you while you sleep. Should you wake, you shall be safe in my arms."

That was like music to her ears. She turned away from him, giving him her back. "Help me out of my dress," she said. "I don't want to ring for Dot."

He worked her buttons. "Were you really going to kiss Irvine?" he asked, a pained edge to his voice. He lifted her gown over her head and dropped it to the floor.

"I don't know," she said, wanting to be honest. She turned to face him. "I imagined it was you who stood before me, so I'm not certain if I would have gone through with it. I hoped the attention of another might finally help me get over you."

He pulled her close again. "If I had seen his lips on yours, I am not certain what I would have done."

Eliza pulled back from him, pushing him away. "And what of you and Lady Preston? You seemed quite friendly with the use of your given names. Was that an attempt to vex me, or did you find your way into her bed?"

He laughed and tried to pull her back to him, but she shoved him away from her. "My love," he started, "Rosina was married to a friend of mine and Ockham's before he died. Nothing more. I'm quite certain her bed won't be empty at this house party, but it has never been me warming it."

She relaxed her shoulders. As much as he would have been driven mad had she been with another man, she wasn't sure what she might have done if she had witnessed him with a woman. They were quite the pair, and she knew their marriage would always be a passionate one. And she couldn't wait to finally become his wife.

"Make love to me, Nick," she whispered, tugging at his cravat. Once she got it loose, she dropped it to the floor.

"You mean I didn't thoroughly satisfy you earlier? I am clearly out of practice," he jested.

She laughed. "You know you did. But we were both hurt and taking what we could from each other then. We weren't even undressed. I wish to be with you now only because of love."

He released a low growl and worked to unlace her stays, then removed them from her body. She unbuttoned his coats and pushed them off his shoulders. He shrugged the rest of the way out of them and tossed them aside before pulling his shirt from his breeches. She unbuttoned a few of his shirt buttons, and he pulled it over his head. Clothes were flying, and their movements were hurried. The need to be in each other's arms was beyond paramount.

She removed her stockings and chemise while he worked his way out of his boots and socks. He refocused his attention on her and began removing pins from her hair. She aided him in the effort and soon her long hair fell down around her shoulders in waves.

When they both stood naked before each other, the emotion of the moment set in and tears escaped her eyes, running down her cheeks.

"I'm so sorry, my love," he said, doing his best to catch her tears with his thumbs. "I'm sorry we lost those years, but we will make the many more we have together the happiest of our lives."

She threw herself into his arms, and he scooped her up, cradling her before he set her gently on the bed. He blew out the candle on the bedside table and crawled into bed next to her, pulling the covers up over them.

Eliza pulled him to settle on top of her. He took her lips in a series of long, deep kisses before he kissed her jaw. "I love you so very much," he whispered against her cheek.

Wrapping her legs around him, she urged him to enter her. "The words 'I love you' don't feel like enough to describe what I feel for you, Nick," she replied. "I fear I shall never leave your side."

He reached his hand between their bodies, and her breath became ragged when he touched her between her legs.

"I fear I shall never allow you to leave our bed," he said.

Nick removed his hand and supported himself with his hands on each side of her head. He entered her slowly, pushing himself all the way inside.

Eliza held him tighter with her legs, reveling in their joining and being as one again. He dipped his head down and took her lips, sweeping his tongue across her bottom lip until she opened for him. Their kiss was as slow and intense as the deep thrusts of his cock. She had missed him so much, missed the love and intimacy they had once shared, and it was as if they picked right back up where they had left off.

"Nick," she moaned. Her fingernails dug into his back, and she pulled him down to rest his weight atop her as he continued to drive her closer to the brink of ecstasy. "Perhaps you don't pull out this time," she whispered in his ear.

"Are you certain?" he asked, his breath frantic.

"I have never been more certain. I wish to be yours in every way and feel the throb of your cock releasing inside of me." He had never done so before besides…in other places. It was the only intimate act they hadn't experienced together.

He increased the intensity of his thrusts, and she could hold back no longer. When she cried out, he pressed his lips against hers to catch her moans. He pumped into her only a couple more times before he reached his climax and spilled his seed with small thrusts deep inside of her, whispering her name before kissing her again.

Nick shifted beside her on the bed and pulled her against him. With her back to his front, he wrapped his arms around her.

"Sleep now, my love," he whispered, moving her hair to the side so he could kiss the back of her neck. "I shall be right here."

She sighed and settled against him and hoped that if it had all been a dream, she would never awaken from it.

Chapter 10

Nick woke up to the intoxicating lavender scent that haunted him in the years he had been apart from Eliza. He nuzzled her hair and inhaled deeply, never happier knowing that he had her back in his arms. She shifted her bottom against him, and his cock sprang to life. She stirred and shifted so she faced him.

"You're here," she said, smiling with her eyes half open. "It wasn't just a wonderful dream."

"I'm here," he said, placing a soft kiss on her lips. "We must dress, though."

She pouted. "What if I don't wish to dress?"

He laughed and kissed her forehead. "Your maid shall arrive at any moment, and we should speak with our hosts as soon as possible," he said before bringing his lips close to her ear. "The sooner we depart, the sooner I can make you come many times in the carriage."

"Promise?" she asked, winking at him.

He released a low growl. "I must make up for lost time."

Nick kissed her again before climbing from the bed and pulling his breeches on. At least if Eliza's maid should knock, he might not completely scandalize her. He grabbed his shirt and wrapped it around himself. He worked the buttons as Eliza threw back the covers, grabbing her dressing robe and tying it around herself.

"I shall change clothes in my chamber and will meet you at the top of the stairs," he said. "Wait for me there."

"I'll be there as quickly as I can," she replied. She stepped around the bed and gave him a quick kiss. The kind of tender, loving kiss they would share many times a day for the rest of their lives.

He grinned at her, acknowledging that he was the luckiest man alive. "Have your maid pack for you so we can depart."

As much as he didn't wish to leave, he turned and cracked the door to check the hallways, then crept out of her chamber. He hurried by the door next to hers but noted he heard a man's and a woman's voices on the other side of the door.

Nick smiled to himself and hurried down the hall. He and Eliza hadn't been the only ones who had a sleepover last night. Their hosts might be scandalized to know so many were taking advantage of their house party to pursue their private entertainment in the night. He made it to the other wing of the house without being seen by anyone and swept into his chamber.

A half hour later, his valet had given him a fresh shave and helped him to dress in fresh clothing. He had informed the man of their travel plans and left him to his work to prepare for their departure. Nick was the first to reach the top of the staircase and waited for his love with his hands clasped behind his back. He rocked on his feet, antsy to have her by his side again. After their time apart, he wasn't certain how long it would take with her at his side before he would no longer feel unease that she might be taken from him.

After another quarter hour, he was rewarded with the beautiful sight of his future wife. She was all smiles, and he rushed to her and brought her hand to his lips. "Are you ready?" he asked.

"Very much so," she replied, smiling up at him with nothing but love in her expression. It reminded him of the many moments they had shared hiding behind her father's stables, where he had first told her he loved her. He meant it then, as much as he still did.

"Then let us find our hosts," he said, offering her his arm. More guests and servants were moving about the halls. A few guests eyed them curiously as Nick and Eliza moved from room to room looking for Lord and Lady Ockham, but thankfully, no one stopped to engage in conversation.

When they couldn't find their hosts anywhere, Nick stopped their butler, Baxter. "Do you know where their lord and ladyship are? We wish to speak with them right away."

"They are in the nursery, my lord," Baxter replied.

"Might you take us to them?" Nick asked. "I had wished to meet their babe."

"Follow me, and I shall check with them," Baxter said.

Nick and Eliza did as the man said and followed him back up the staircase to the family wing where the nursery was. Baxter motioned for them to wait there while he knocked on the door and entered the nursery. He returned in a few moments and waved Nick and Eliza into the room.

"Craven," Ockham said. "This is quite a surprise but do come and meet our son."

Nick laughed to himself at the pride radiating from his friend as he bounced his son in his arms. He hoped Eliza was already carrying their babe. He would adore a sweet babe who looked like their mother. Nick stepped closer to the sleeping babe and smiled down at him. The boy very much favored his father.

"So are you going to tell us what this is about?" Lady Ockham asked, smirking and motioning towards Nick and Eliza. Ockham set his son to rest in the crib.

Nick took Eliza's hand in his. "I'd like to introduce you to the woman I've been pining after."

Their hosts' jaws dropped, and Nick fought his laughter.

"But," Lady Ockham started, "you said she had married someone else. I am not aware that Lady Eliza has ever been married."

"A cruel lie from my father," Nick said. "It seems both of our fathers wished to keep us apart. They hated each other, and we were manipulated by both of them."

Ockham patted his friend on the back. "I'm happy for you that you've worked it out. You are far happier than I've seen you in a long time."

"Thank you," Nick replied. "We wish to wed right away, so we hope you won't be upset with us that we wish to depart today. We have lost far too much time together already."

Lady Ockham stepped close to Eliza and gave her a tight hug and then patted Nick's arm. "Of course not. Hopefully, we shall see you both after you have settled into married life."

Ockham caught his wife's attention. "I guess this means we both lose."

Nick and Eliza eyed him curiously.

"What are you on about, Ockham?" Nick asked.

"We attempted to guess who had captured your heart, but we were only considering married ladies of the *ton*," the man said, shrugging his shoulders.

"Actually, I believe I still win. I did have Lady Eliza at the top of my list of prospects for you," she said to Nick before focusing her attention on her husband. "So that is a win for me, my love."

Ockham rolled his eyes, but his smile was one of mirth.

"Well," Nick started, "we might not have found our way to each other again had it not been for your house party, so we are eternally grateful." Nick held out his hand to his friend for a shake.

Ockham shook his hand and then wrapped his arm around his wife.

Nick and Eliza said their goodbyes to their hosts, as well as the sleeping babe, and then departed. On their way to the staircase, they passed by Eliza's chamber and then the door next to hers opened. Eliza's friend, Juliet, exited the room.

"Oh," she said, startled by the two of them. Then a confused expression formed. "What happened here?"

Interesting she should ask that, given that Nick very clearly heard a man's voice coming from her room, but that was of no matter to him.

Eliza reached for her friend's hand. "Nick and I are to marry. We are departing now to do so and take up residence at our country estate."

"What?" Juliet asked, shocked. "How did this come to be?"

Nick could tell from the lady's reaction that she wasn't certain if she trusted him with Eliza.

"Things weren't as they seemed. We were both tricked," Eliza quickly explained. "I shall share all the details soon, but we must depart. I hope you won't hate me for leaving you to enjoy the party without me. I hope you shan't be bored once I am gone."

"I am sure I shall manage," Juliet said, smiling at her friend.

I'm sure she will, Nick thought to himself.

"I am so happy for you, truly," Juliet exclaimed, wrapping her arms around Eliza. Juliet shifted her focus to Nick. "I look forward to getting to know you, too, my lord."

"Nick, please," he said. "I'm sure we will see you often."

"But not for at least a few weeks," Eliza said, staring at her friend pointedly. "We won't be accepting callers for a while."

The ladies laughed and hugged each other again. Nick and Eliza escaped the house and requested their carriages without being stopped by any of the other guests. They didn't wish to explain their situation to anyone else just then.

Their trunks were being brought and loaded onto one of Nick's carriages. They requested that Eliza's carriage be sent back to her father with only a message that she wouldn't return. He could stew for a while and wonder what had occurred. The man deserved far worse.

A quarter hour later, they found themselves seated beside each other in their carriage. Once they started their journey, Nick released the ties that held the curtains so they could shut out the rest of the world and focus on each other.

"You certainly don't intend to waste any time, do you?" Eliza asked, giggling.

"Not a single second," he replied, pulling her close to kiss her.

She kissed his jaw and licked the lobe of his ear before whispering, "Good, because it's my turn to remind you to whom you belong."

There was no question, but he would happily play her game and stop in the first village to purchase a jar of oil.

Epilogue

TWO MONTHS LATER

Eliza couldn't believe how happy she was after spending the last few years in a continual state of pain and heartbreak. She smiled so much every day that sometimes her face hurt. She woke up every morning and fell asleep every evening in Nick's arms, just as it always should have been.

She settled into running their household, and Nick handled the estate matters as needed, but they spent much of their time together. They went for walks around their estate, he laid his head in her lap while she read, and they christened just about every room and piece of furniture in the house. He kept his word to ensure they made up for lost time and that he filled their days with love and joy.

After they left the house party, they purchased a special license and married that same day. Then they retired to their county home, adjacent to her father's estate.

Eliza waited for two weeks before she wrote to her father. She needed to calm her ire over the situation and she didn't want to mar their newly wedded bliss with thinking about what to write to the man. When she finally did, she informed him that she had married Nick and that if he ever wanted a chance to know her or her children, he would not only sign over her dowry but would sign a contract stating that the stream belonged to her and Nick. It was the location where they had first met, and too much had already been lost from the ongoing feud. Her father didn't deserve to claim it after what he had done.

She also didn't hesitate to remind him that they possessed many influential friends and would ensure that he received the cut direct from everyone they knew if he didn't comply.

Her father didn't reply to her demands right away, but after a couple of weeks, they were surprised to find that he complied with all of her requests. She couldn't be certain how much influence her mother might have played in that decision, but she was glad to have the matter finally done.

She hadn't quite been ready to forgive him, but she and Nick both agreed to try. Eliza missed her mother and would like to have a relationship with her. They would attend dinner at her parents' home the very next week, in an attempt to begin working on things.

Eliza kicked her dangling feet against the side of his desk as she sat on the edge of it and watched him reply to his correspondence. She often sat with him while he worked as they still struggled to be apart from each other.

"Am I supposed to take that as a hint that you are ready for me to be finished?" Nick asked.

"I wish to go for a ride," she replied, faking a pout.

He dropped his quill. "Well, why didn't you say so?" he asked, leaning back in his chair. "I am right here."

She swatted at his arm. "A ride to the hunting cabin, you vexing man."

"Well, lead the way, wife," he replied, faking his own pout.

"You'll enjoy it," she said. "I promise." She hopped off his desk and grabbed his hand to pull him with her to the stables. Their horses were saddled and ready, just as she had requested.

They raced each other to the hunting cabin, and when they arrived, he hopped to the ground and then lifted her down. It wasn't lost on her how he intentionally set her down so that she slid against his body. She pressed up on her toes to reward his efforts with a quick kiss.

She clasped his hand and pulled him with her into the cabin.

"What is all of this?" he asked, looking around the room in amazement.

A fire had already been set in the main room. Roses and candles had been placed around the room. Eliza proceeded to light each of the candles. A light supper had been set up for them on the sideboard, just as she had requested.

Nick came up behind her and wrapped his arms around her waist. "You didn't answer me, my love."

She turned in his arms to face him. "We have so many fond memories here, and I wish to make more."

He responded by pulling her against him and kissing her, sweeping his tongue into her mouth to massage it with hers. She kissed him with all the love and desire she felt in her heart, edging him backward towards the settee before the fire. Pushing him back on it, she straddled him.

"I have a surprise for you, my love," she said, placing a sweet kiss on his neck. Followed by several more kisses.

He shifted her skirts so he could get his hand underneath them and released a low growl when his fingers rubbed against her already wet folds. "Is it that you aren't wearing your stays?" he asked. "Because I quite like that surprise."

She shook her head.

"Hmmm," he murmured, thinking. He slipped two fingers inside of her and her head fell back. "Is it that you are very ready for me?" he asked. "Because I like that surprise even better."

She looked into his eyes and shook her head again.

Nick unbuttoned his falls, his large shaft protruding between them. She stroked him a few times before he lifted her hips so she could guide him inside of her.

She rocked on him, both of them panting in need.

"Is this my surprise?" he asked. "Because this is the best of all."

She shook her head again, moaning.

He gripped her hips and helped her to ride him. Eliza wrapped her arms around his neck, holding him close as he thrust upwards inside of her, entering her so deeply she released a steady stream of moans. She sucked and licked his neck and jaw while she rode him with such intensity that drove them both towards the edge of ecstasy. After several more thrusts, she cried out against his lips when she shattered in his arms. He bucked and thrust beneath her until he released himself deep inside of her. She fell against him and he wrapped his arms around her, stroking her hair, his cock half-erect still inside of her.

"I am out of guesses," he said. "What is my surprise?"

She sat up and clasped his cheeks with her hands. "I'm carrying our sweet babe."

"What?" he exclaimed. "Are you certain?"

She nodded, tears forming at the corners of her eyes.

He placed his hand on her stomach. Her heart pounded with more love than she could have imagined when his own eyes welled with tears. She kissed the corner of his right eye, tasting his salty tear on her lips.

"I love you so much, Eliza," he said.

"I love you, Nick," she said, shedding a few happy tears down her own cheeks.

"I hope you know you have made me the happiest man in the entire world. Again," he said, wiping her tears and turning more serious. "But I don't want you going for rides any longer. I won't take any chances with either of you." He tenderly rubbed her stomach again.

She rocked on his lap and gave him a wicked smile when she could feel the intensity of his reaction inside of her as he grew hard again.

"As long as you are only speaking of horseback riding, I shall agree," she said, "because this"—she rode him harder—"I won't give this up."

Want more of Nick and Eliza?

Visit https://dl.bookfunnel.com/iwmybfkwbb to receive an auto-download of another scene in their married life together and join my mailing list! Meet the kids, find out if they are still as hot for each other as they have always been, and see what's coming next for them!

Here is a look at the full series, and keep reading for a sneak peek at the next book!

The Unlikely Betrothal Series

A different couple at the same house party finds their match! Who will be next? Each of these books are stand-alone stories complete with a HEA and lots of spice, but recommended reading order is below:

Book 1: The Earl and the Vixen

Book 2: The Rake and the Muse

Book 3: The Marquess and the Earl

Book 4: The Viscount and the Wallflower

Book 5: The Duke and the Widow

Dearest Reader

T hank you for taking the time to read The Earl and the Vixen! I hope you enjoyed this spicy read, which is the first book in my Unlikely Betrothal series. I enjoyed bringing Nick and Eliza's story to life on the page and can't wait to introduce you to the other couples at the Ockhams' house party!

I am so thankful for all my readers and would appreciate it if you would leave an honest review on sites like Amazon, Goodreads, BookBub, etc.! Also, I'd love to stay in touch, so please visit christinadianebooks.com to join my mailing list and receive a free copy of Only A Rake Will Do (the Ockhams are in that one, too!), and stay informed on upcoming releases, promotions, and current projects.

If you are interested in being on my permanent ARC team and/or Street Team, send me a message on one of my socials! I'd love to chat!

I hope all of you will follow me and get the latest happenings and info on releases from my historical romance friends on any of my socials:

- Website: christinadianebooks.com

- Instagram: @christinadianeauthor

- Facebook: christinadiane

- TikTok: @christinadianeauthor

- YouTube: @ChristinaDianeAuthor

- Twitter: @CDianeAuthor

- GoodReads: ChristinaDiane

- Follow Me on Amazon: Christina Diane

- Follow Me onBookBub: Christina Diane

- Join my Reader Group: The Swoonworthy Scoundrels Society

Hopefully I left you wanting more, so keep reading for a sneak peek at what is coming in *The Rake and the Muse*, book two in the Unlikely Betrothal series! I hope you are as excited as I am for Theo and Juliet! You can also go ahead and get your copy of The Rake and the Muse https://books2read.com/therakeandthemuse!

The Rake and the Muse

LONDON, ENGLAND - SPRING 1813

Juliet Lane, the only child of the Earl of Avon, hid in the retiring room at the Fletchers' ball, doing her best to catch her breath after she practically sprinted down the hall. The retiring room seemed like the only place she might avoid getting asked to dance by any other gentleman with wandering hands. After what she had experienced on the dance floor with Lord Dunblane, she didn't much feel like dancing for the rest of the evening if she could help it.

Rejecting a dance with a gentleman just wasn't done, which left her vulnerable to such partners if she remained in the ballroom. Lord Dunblane took it upon himself to grasp her bottom during each of the turns so that no one might notice. When his hands weren't glued to her arse, his eyes were trained on her bosom. Which was hard to cover with the style of her dress and the way her stays positioned her ample breasts and made them appear even larger, if that were possible. She regretted that she hadn't worn a fichu and wouldn't ever make the same mistake again.

She was used to men staring at her, undressing her with their eyes. It was a usual occurrence at ton events. Juliet didn't possess the small body of the other misses on the Marriage Mart. They salivated and hardly noticed her face, let alone anything she might have to say, once they took notice of her body. Her figure was shaped more like an hourglass, with an abundant pair of full breasts and curvy hips, with a shapely arse.

The sound of voices reached her as someone approached the room, and she resolved to remain in her hiding place behind the screen.

"She probably went home," one young lady said. Juliet didn't recognize her voice and didn't dare peek her head out to see who it was.

"It makes you wonder," another lady started, "how the modiste has enough fabric to fashion a dress for those hips."

Both of the ladies laughed, proud of themselves. It wasn't anything Juliet hadn't heard before and she could only assume they were speaking about her.

In truth, the modiste had a terrible time fashioning dresses that were in high fashion because of her shape—not because of lack of fabric, but due to the current fashions, Juliet thought to herself. It was deuced annoying.

"Well, the gentlemen seem taken with her. It makes me wonder if we should start stuffing tissue paper into our stays."

"They shall never marry her. Wishing to dally with a woman and marrying her are quite different."

The ladies laughed again.

Juliet sensed another person had exited the screened area beside hers. "Lady Theodosia," another unique voice started. "There is nary a man alive who would wish to do either with you."

"You are one to talk," the one Juliet assumed to be Lady Theodosia said. "And where exactly is your husband, Lady Eliza?"

"Hopefully he doesn't exist," the voice sounding again like Lady Eliza replied. "Although, based on the three marriage offers I declined last week, perhaps I'll see if one of those heartbroken gentlemen might be desperate enough to saddle themselves to you."

Juliet covered her mouth to fight her laughter behind the screen. She didn't enjoy mocking others, but the lady certainly deserved a set down.

"Come, Rebecca," Lady Theodosia said. "We don't need to be seen with such company."

Once Juliet was certain the ladies had left, she emerged from her hiding place and the woman she believed could only be Lady Eliza was still in the room.

"Thank you for that," Juliet said, offering a small smile to the woman.

Lady Eliza shifted her attention to her and appeared surprised to find her standing there. Her expression shifted to a kind smile. "I can't stand those two," Lady Eliza replied. "Don't worry about them. They just envy the attention you get."

"I don't even want it," Juliet said, deciding to forgo the usual social protocol of feigning indifference and speak honestly with the lady who'd just come to her rescue. "I'm Lady Juliet, by the way."

"So glad to meet you. I'm Lady Eliza," the woman replied. "But please, just call me Eliza."

Juliet nodded in agreement.

"I don't much care for the attention either," Eliza shared. "I am uncertain if I ever wish to wed."

Juliet noted a pain in the woman's expression and assumed there was a reason for Eliza to make such a declaration, when she was almost certain it was the lady's first season out. Although, it was also Juliet's first season, and she shared a similar position on marriage.

"Would you like to come to tea at my house tomorrow?" Juliet asked, staring down at her feet. "I don't have many friends, and it would be nice to talk to someone who isn't as haughty as some of these other debutantes."

Eliza looped her arm in Juliet's. "I'd be delighted."

"Who did you say was joining for tea today?" Juliet's father, Earl of Avon, asked.

"Lady Eliza," Juliet replied. "The Earl of Nelson's daughter."

Her father nodded his approval. "I am glad to see you making friends, princess. You should find the season much more enjoyable without only your aunt to keep you company."

The previous evening had already been much more fun with Eliza at her side. They avoided most of the gentlemen, and they talked and laughed the evening away. The pair had become fast friends, and Juliet couldn't wait to learn more about her new friend and to entertain a guest for tea.

"I agree, Papa. You needn't join us, though. I'm sure we would just bore you with all the lady-like talk."

He laughed and patted her shoulder. "I shall make myself scarce. I hope you have an enjoyable time." Her father kissed the top of her head and then started for his study.

Juliet adored her father. Since her mother had passed when she was a young girl, he was all she had. She just didn't prefer him to linger around and listen to her conversations, especially the first time she'd have a friend come to call.

"My lady," her butler said, "you have a caller. Lady Eliza is here to see you."

"Thank you, White," she replied. "Please show her in here and bring tea."

He bowed and in a matter of moments, returned with Eliza.

"Juliet," she said, coming right to her and bussing her cheeks. "I am so glad to see you."

"Please, take a seat. Tea will be in shortly."

Eliza took the seat in the chair right next to where Juliet sat on the settee.

When Eliza glanced up at the wall, Juliet followed her gaze to see the paintings that she fixed her gaze on. "Who painted those? They are quite beautiful."

Juliet grinned and glanced at the paintings, pride radiating from her. "I did."

"You painted those?" Eliza asked, impressed. "You are talented, indeed."

A maid entered and rolled in the tea cart, interrupting their conversation. Once the maid departed, Juliet prepared them each a cup of tea.

Once they had their refreshments, Eliza stared at the paintings again. "Could you paint me?"

"I am certain I could," Juliet said.

"Your paintings should be in a gallery," Eliza said, her tone serious.

Juliet huffed. "I tried that, and the gallery wasn't interested in art from a woman, especially one from beau monde."

"How dare they!" Eliza exclaimed. Juliet couldn't agree more. Just another reason she and Eliza got on so well.

"I hope to open my own gallery one day. A gallery that will accept all work, regardless of gender, race, or class."

Eliza clasped her hands at her chest. "I love that! I shall be happy to help with your endeavor if I can. But I'm afraid I have no artistic abilities besides singing and the pianoforte."

"Just having your support is enough," Juliet said, beaming at her friend. "It shall be difficult to find others who will support the gallery, but I am determined."

"I have no doubt you shall succeed, Juliet," Eliza said, taking a sip of her tea. "You never told me why you were hiding in the bathroom last night."

Juliet huffed. "There are gentlemen who can't seem to keep their hands off certain places on my body."

Eliza rolled her eyes. "Just like a man to do whatever he wishes, with no concern for anyone else."

Juliet agreed, of course, but assumed her friend had different reasons for believing so.

Juliet contemplated Eliza's reaction. "Why is it you don't wish to wed?"

"I fancied myself in love once, and that was a farce," Eliza replied. "I have no desire to go through that again."

"What happened, if you don't mind me asking?" Juliet took a sip of her tea, awaiting the answer.

Eliza drew a deep breath. "I shall tell you the full story soon. I promise. Let us speak of more pleasant things today."

"I ask because I am uncertain a husband will support my artistic ventures, but I am so dreadfully curious about other benefits a marriage brings." She had tried to get her maid to tell her of such things to no avail.

Eliza laughed and gave her a knowing look. "Oh, I believe I understand your meaning."

Juliet's face flushed. "I don't care for these entitled men who grope me in ballrooms, but it might be nice to experience such things with a gentleman of interest. Whatever those things may be. With Mama gone, I shan't ask Papa to explain it to me."

"If that is what you wish to know, I can explain such things," Eliza said, grinning at her friend behind her teacup. "And I can tell you how to please yourself with no need of a man."

Acknowledgments

There are so many amazing people in my life who have supported me, new and old. Authors and readers! I truly appreciate each and every one of you and hope that you will continue to stick with me on this journey. I would like to call out a few key people, but please know that this isn't an exhaustive list and there are so many people whom I love and adore. I wish that I had room to name them all!

Steve: My husband is the one who continually supports my big and daring dreams, all while providing tech support, cooking dinner, doing the laundry, spitballing ideas with me, and so much more! He's a true partner in every extent of the word and I couldn't do any of it without him. Love you, Babe!

Dexter and Felix: My boys frequently provide me with distractions while I'm in the middle of writing. However, they are also often the inspiration for some of the witty sibling banter that makes it into my drafts. I don't even know what they're going to think when they realize one day that their mother writes smut. Oh well... I love you, boys!

Rachel, Nina & Brittany: I am fortunate to have these ladies (my mom, aunt, and sister) in my life. They have been there for me the entire way and have supported me through the ups and downs throughout the years. They are all used to my crazy ideas and what I can do when I put my mind to something. They just keep cheering me on. They are the ones who hold all of my embarrassing stories and memories, so I can't ever let anyone speak to them without me present. But I love you, all!

Erin: We were destined to be besties from our very first meeting. She is the person I talk to about all the things when I need to bounce around ideas, work on my mindset, take a breath, and so much more! Love you, dearly!

Morgan: None of this could be possible without her keeping the trains moving! If there is something with this biz that needs to get done, she is right there at my side helping move it forward, and she usually comes up with a simpler, better idea! Truly, thank you!!!

Bliss: I can't believe the good fortune we had to have met in a smutty follow train group on Insta, but here we are! It was another fateful moment! I would be sad without our daily texts, talking about our writing progress, smutty scenes, and all the happenings in life. Thank you so much!!!

Courtney: Fate struck again, and I am so thankful to have a partner in crime and twinsie for this author journey! Thanks for all of the ideating, chats, and feedback into the wee hours of the morning! We are going to rock this thing!

Thank you to everyone on my Beta, ARC, and Street Team! (Especially Rachel W., she has literally read every single word that I have written, and I haven't scared her away yet!) The love and care that you put into reading, providing feedback, and helping promote the stories means so much more to me than you know. I hope we get to keep hanging out together for many years to come!

Thank you to Dragonblade Publishing for seeing something in me and my stories! I know I am going to continue to grow in my author career with your guidance and support.

Thank you to all of the amazing author friends and influencers I have met through various social media groups! This amazing community has seriously been one of the best parts of this whole journey, and I am thankful you all let me be a part of it!

About the Author

Christina Diane is a wife and mother who enjoys weaving stories of love and passion from her home in Northern Maine. She is a hybrid indie and traditionally published author with Dragonblade Publishing. Her favorite genre to read and write is historical romance set in the Regency era. She also reads many other genres, especially dark romances and psychological thrillers.

When she is not writing or chasing after her family, she usually has a Kindle in her hand! Along with her husband and two boys, her family includes their three French bulldogs who go everywhere with them, as well as two solid black cats. The entire family is always up for new adventures.

Her writing journey began at the age of nine when she created her own comic strip, Grizzly Grouch. In adulthood, she was a freelance writer for several years, mostly writing lifestyle pieces for blogs. She found that she couldn't stop thinking about stories and characters, so much that she had to get them on the page! Christina frequently has dreams of random character ARCs that go into a massive list of planned writings. She currently has more than ten series just waiting to be written!

Aside from her family, writing, and books, she loves *Bridgerton*, the Grinch, Jessica Rabbit, horror movies, Chucky dolls, cold brew, yoga, *Hamilton*, the color pink, and speaking in obscure quotes from movies and TV shows.

Christina loves chatting with her readers and talking about great reads, so please contact her on socials! She'd love to hear what you think about her books and what you'd love to see more of!

Printed in Great Britain
by Amazon

55966484R00088